P9-CRV-662

Mrs. Pollifax
and the
Second Thief

Mrs. Pollifax
and the Second Thief

DOROTHY GILMAN

LARGE PRINT BOOK CLUB EDITION

Doubleday

NEW YORK   LONDON   TORONTO   SYDNEY   AUCKLAND

This Large Print Edition, prepared especially for Doubleday Book & Music Clubs, Inc., contains the complete, unabridged text of the original Publisher's Edition.

PUBLISHED BY DOUBLEDAY
a division of Bantam Doubleday
Dell Publishing Group, Inc.
1540 Broadway, New York, New York 10036

DOUBLEDAY and the portrayal of an anchor with a dolphin are trademarks of Doubleday, a division of Bantam Doubleday Dell Publishing Group, Inc.

**This Large Print Book carries the
Seal of Approval of N.A.V.H.**

to Alejandro Butters

Mrs. Pollifax
and the
Second Thief

1

Mrs. Pollifax stood under a dripping umbrella and wondered why it so often rained at funerals. Or at burials, she amended, staring out from under her umbrella at sodden flowers heaped around the grave, and a dozen figures in black, heads bowed as the words *ashes to ashes, dust to dust* were intoned. She too was in black, wearing a veil that scratched her nose and made her very much want to sneeze; resisting this compulsion she gripped her purse more firmly in front of her with both hands and moved edgily to the left and then to the right. From the look of the sullen gray sky overhead she guessed the gentle rain was about to become a downpour, and at the same time she realized the last prayer was over and the figures around the grave were stirring, eyes opening, heads turning.

A man to one side of Mrs. Pollifax glanced at her and said, "A sad day."

"Yes," she said. She gave him an appropriately wan smile from behind her veil and opened her purse to tuck away her handkerchief. There seemed nothing more to do, and with a last glance at the group of mourners, separating now into individuals of various shapes and sexes, she detached herself and walked away, slowly threading her way among the tombstones toward the graveled road that wound through the cemetery. Passing the hearse and a line of cars she continued toward a limousine that had pulled up under the dripping trees at a distance from the others.

Seeing her approach, a chauffeur in uniform emerged from the limousine to open the door. Taking the umbrella she handed him, he snapped it shut, bowed, and once she was settled inside he walked smartly around the car to seat himself behind the wheel. A moment later, the car in motion, he said over his shoulder, "Go all right?"

"My purse made odd little clicking sounds every time I snapped a picture," she told him, "but I think the rain on the umbrella covered it up."

"Good," said Bishop, assistant to Carstairs of the CIA, and he pressed his foot to the accelerator. "I suggest we get the hell out of here and back to headquarters so Carstairs can brief you on where you're going, and why."

"Not to mention whose funeral I just attended," she said tartly, and since Bishop seemed determined not to explain anything yet she sat back and wondered if Cyrus had reached Chicago yet.

She had begun the day with Cyrus, who was leaving for Chicago on a 9:30 A.M. plane: his nephew Jimmy was heading the defense team for the biggest murder trial of the season and he had begged his uncle to bring his legal expertise to Chicago for consultations and support. Mrs. Pollifax had planned to join him in a week, once the trial was underway—or so she had assumed until Bishop's hurried phone call at half-past six that morning.

"No time for small talk," he'd said quickly. "We've had an SOS from John Sebastian Farrell in Europe, asking for you and Cyrus by tomorrow noon."

Momentarily stunned she had said, "Farrell's working for you again? But at Christmas he wrote that he was back in Mexico City—rescuing the art gallery he had to abandon when his cover was blown."

"Explanations later," said Bishop. "Can you and Cyrus head for Europe tonight?"

"Cyrus can't," she blurted out. "Cyrus, are you there?"

"Yes, m'dear," he said from the extension phone in the living room.

"He's leaving for Chicago in three hours," she explained. "For the Bates murder trial, I'm driving him to the airport in twenty minutes. His nephew's defending Bates."

"Your nephew's James Reed, Cyrus? Chip off the old block, obviously. But that means—look here," Bishop said desperately, "can one of you still go? You, for instance? This is *Farrell*."

She'd said, "Well, Cyrus? Still on the phone?"

"I'm here. Always said I'd never interfere," growled Cyrus, "but damn it, Bishop, I've every right to insist she not go alone. What sort of trouble's he in?"

"No idea," said Bishop, "and he's *not* working for us, but we owe him and an SOS is an SOS. Look," he added, "if Emily can go I've an idea Carstairs will know exactly the person to go with her, in fact I can guess who it would be, a well-trained and knowledgeable agent, I promise."

"I'll worry like hell—as usual," said Cyrus, "but I'm fond of Farrell, too. Can you pack in twenty minutes, Emily?"

"In fifteen," she said eagerly, "and if you weren't in the living room, Cyrus, I'd give you a hug."

"That too has to wait," said Bishop. "Start packing, there'll be a private plane for you at the airport when you deliver Cyrus and you'll be paged."

Now, seven hours later, Mrs. Pollifax had progressed no further than Virginia, where she had been presented with a black coat and hat and sent off to a mysterious funeral to take photographs, she was in a limousine with Bishop being driven back to headquarters to learn where she was to go, why Farrell wasn't in Mexico City where he was supposed to be, and what a funeral had to do with his being in enough trouble to send an SOS to the Department. She thought crossly that it was like a treasure hunt, this being rushed from place to place with no idea why, but it was now two o'clock in the afternoon and high time to unravel this confusing skein of events.

"Are we nearly there?" she asked. "I hesitate to mention it but I am cold and *wet,* Bishop."

"One more mile," said Bishop, "and I might point out the heater in this elegant stretch-limo is defective—in a word, it doesn't work—and I'm cold, too."

Mrs. Pollifax couldn't resist a pointed, "A private plane, a limousine, someone to take Cyrus' place, and a trip to Europe, all this for Farrell when he's not working for you?"

Over his shoulder Bishop said indignantly, "You know damn well we want him *back;* he's not even forty-five yet, he's too young to retire. Naturally we're hoping you'll emphasize the lengths to which we're going to give him aid and comfort. We *miss* him.''

So do I, thought Mrs. Pollifax, and smiled as she remembered her first meeting with Farrell in Mexico not long ago. How shocked she had been to find herself shackled to a man who resembled a hero in a cheap B-movie! A handsome and reckless-looking adventurer, she had thought disapprovingly, being at that time fresh from her Garden Club in New Brunswick, New Jersey, and not yet accustomed to being drugged, kidnapped, and tied to a post with a stranger. Following this introduction they had experienced a very educational two weeks in a prison cell in Albania, during which she had puzzled out how to escape with a badly wounded Farrell and with the mysterious stranger in the adjoining cell. The fact that she had accomplished this with some élan—or so thought Carstairs— had proved the beginning of a number of adventures and a new career to which she had to admit she had become addicted.

Now she wondered who on earth Carstairs could find at such short notice to accompany her to Europe, and she fervently

hoped he would find no one; she also wondered why Farrell was there at all when she
remembered so clearly the business card
that he'd enclosed with his Christmas note:
Signor J. Sebastian Farrell, Galería des
Artes & Antiguallas, Calle el Siglo 20, Mexico City. . . .

Twenty minutes later they were entering
Bishop's office high up in the CIA building,
where he reached out a hand, saying, "I'll
deliver the camera to the lab now and be
right back."

Removing the black coat, Mrs. Pollifax
reached into her shoulder purse and ex-
tracted from its depths the smaller purse
that had accompanied her to the funeral.
"Ingenious bit of trickery," she said, handing it to him.

"Ah, but we deal in trickery here," he said
with a grin. Carefully placing the purse in a
plastic bag he pointed to the inner door.
"Just walk in, Carstairs is expecting you.
And there's hot coffee," he called over his
shoulder before he disappeared into the
hall.

Mrs. Pollifax, shivering, murmured, "Positively ambrosial." Opening the door she

walked into Carstairs' office, a quite familiar room by now, and found him already pouring coffee.

"Delighted to see you," he said, handing her a steaming cup. "Damnably cold for early May. Cream? Sugar?"

"Black, thank you." Watching him as he moved to sit down at his desk she thought that he'd changed scarcely at all since the day she'd been given her first job as a simple courier; he really ought to look harassed and worn, considering all the intrigues he'd masterminded, and she said accusingly, "You should look *older.*"

Amused, he said, "I *am* older. Would it make you happy if I admit to a touch of arthritis in my left knee?"

She said warmly, "It would, frankly, it provides the human touch. Now about this funeral—"

"That can wait," he told her. "Bishop's explained that during the night we had an SOS from Farrell asking for you and Cyrus as soon as possible?"

She nodded. "Yes, but not why, or where, and Bishop said he's not working for you?"

Carstairs sighed. "Unfortunately, no . . . Stubborn chap. He's been busy with that art gallery in Mexico City, or he was until four days ago when we heard from him. At that time he phoned from Europe to ask two things of us: one, if we had any information in our files about a rather mysterious collector of art who had just hired him to pursue —for a great deal of money—a particularly rare document, and—ah, here's Bishop."

"They'll have the photos enlarged for us in fifteen minutes," Bishop announced, pouring himself a cup of coffee. "Sorry for the interruption, pray go on."

"What sort of rare document, did Farrell say?" asked Mrs. Pollifax.

"Oh yes. Nothing political involved here, it was a straightforward inquiry and we owe Farrell that. It seemed that his collector, name of Ambrose Vica, had been told of a document discovered in Sicily bearing the signature of Julius Caesar. A real find, if authentic, since no signature of Julius Caesar has ever been discovered."

"Good heavens, Sicily?"

Carstairs nodded. "Yes. Both his earlier

inquiry by phone and his SOS cable last night came from Sicily."

"So that's where I'm headed!"

Bishop nodded. "Plane out of Kennedy airport tonight, change at Milan, and arrival in morning at Palermo's Punta Raisi airport. And just out of curiosity," he added with a grin, "tell me the first word that comes to your mind when I say 'Sicily.' Free-association, no cheating!"

"Slip-fingered Eddy," she said at once, and seeing Bishop's astonishment she explained in a kind voice, "Eddy was Cyrus' favorite criminal, a small-time burglar who Cyrus sentenced more than a dozen times before retiring from the bench. He told Slip-fingered Eddy over and over and over that he was never cut out to be a criminal—he botched every job he tried—but Eddy just assured him that he'd try harder next time."

Bishop said, "That wasn't the answer I expected."

"So I noticed," she said with a twinkle.

"Was he Sicilian?"

"Born there, yes."

Bishop sighed. "You've ruined my theory

on stereotypes; most people say 'Sicily? Oh, the Mafia.' "

Carstairs leaned back in his chair and smiled. "Actually there's a great deal more to Sicily than any Mafia. It was occupied and fought over by the Phoenicians, Carthaginians, Greeks, Romans, Vandals, and—according to Farrell—Julius Caesar personally launched his attack on Africa in 47 B.C. from the town of Lilybaeum, now called Marsala. It's quite possible that if such a document exists it could have— *might* have—been found there."

"And now he's in trouble, but what can have happened?" Grasping at straws she said, "What did you find out about this Ambrose Vica who hired him?"

"That he's a wealthy collector," Carstairs said smoothly, "and not—as possibly Farrell wondered—Mafia-connected."

"Is he Sicilian?"

"No, but he has a villa in Sicily near Palermo, as well as a home in Mexico City, and in Paris, and an apartment in Rome."

"And Farrell would know about authenticating such things as a signature by Julius Caesar?"

Carstairs smiled. "He's certainly equipped to expose a forgery. Before you met him he'd built up quite a reputation at his gallery for authenticating old paintings and restoring those of value."

"A man of many talents, yes," murmured Mrs. Pollifax, "but this SOS?"

Carstairs put down his coffee cup and nodded. "It arrived by cable, and it read, if I remember correctly—" He closed his eyes a moment and recited, "URGENTLY BEG POLLIFAX AND REED SOONEST STOP MIDDAY PUBLIC SQUARE ERICE SICILY DEFINITELY WITH HIRED CAR MAYDAY MAYDAY SOS LOVE TO ALL FARRELL."

"He must be in hiding," said Mrs. Pollifax. "I don't like the sound of it, do you? But you mentioned his asking two things of you in his phone call to you four days ago: information on Ambrose Vica and—?"

Bishop answered this one. "That's where the funeral and the photographs come in— that was his second request. He asked for photos of those attending the funeral of a Mrs. Estelle Blaise in Reston, Virginia. He emphasized that it was very important but with no explanation as to why. We had to do a hell of a lot of work to find the right funeral home. His SOS, of course, came only last night, you understand. Now, of course, you can deliver the photos to him personally."

"You know no more than this?" she asked suspiciously.

Carstairs smiled at Mrs. Pollifax. "I needn't remind you that Farrell was one of our agents for nearly twenty years, and a damn good one, and we'd dearly like to have him work with us again. You might say we've extended him the courtesy of not pressing for explanations, always hopeful that he can be persuaded to come back to us."

A somewhat devious reply, thought Mrs. Pollifax, but she smiled back at him. "Then I think I'd like to change now into my own clothes and ask how"—she glanced at her watch—"how I reach New York."

Bishop smiled. "Royally. Private plane again, directly to Kennedy."

"And—I assume alone?" she asked at last.

Carstairs and Bishop exchanged glances. "To Sicily, yes," said Carstairs tactfully, "but you'll be met at Punta Raisi airport by someone who knows the island and will have hired a car."

She said resentfully, "And just who—?"

"Your suitcase is in the other room," Bishop told her cheerfully, "and you'll be restored to that dashing red-feathered hat you arrived in." When she gave him a stormy glance he added meekly, "Agent's name is Rossiter. And it will be all right. After all, you don't speak or understand Italian, do you?"

Taken aback by this, since it was quite true, Mrs. Pollifax rose from her chair and said with dignity, "If you'll lend me a closet, then, to change my clothes, please."

Carstairs rose, too, but he had not finished with her yet. He said firmly, "We want to be as supportive as possible, Mrs. Pollifax. This obviously has nothing to do with the Department but it's the Department that's lending you to Farrell and we'd like you to keep in touch. You still have the confidential cable and phone numbers by way of Baltimore?" When she nodded he said, "Good, have a fine trip then and give Farrell our regards."

Carstairs watched Bishop and Mrs. Pollifax leave. Reminding himself that he'd now completed his obligations to Farrell he returned to the intelligence reports waiting for him on his desk. To his surprise he found it difficult to concentrate; he had not previously wondered what a funeral and photos had to do with the rumored discovery of Julius Caesar's signature, and about what possibly could have driven Farrell into hiding, if Mrs. Pollifax's surmise was correct. There was Ambrose Vica, too, about whom he had not been entirely forthcoming, even though their dossier on him was only two sentences in length. He frowned and returned to the intelligence reports, but after struggling with errant thoughts for half an hour he rang the buzzer for Bishop.

"Has Mrs. Pollifax left?" he asked.

"On her way to Kennedy, yes," said Bishop.

"Do we have duplicates of the photographs she's taking to Farrell?"

"Yes, they're on my desk, I'll bring them in."

Together they looked over the dozen people that Mrs. Pollifax had photographed, each one enlarged now, but they meant nothing to Carstairs. No face brought a gasp of recognition, there were no hints or clues, and yet Carstairs couldn't suppress a growing feeling of unease.

Puzzled, he said, "She captured on film everyone at the burial?"

Bishop nodded. "She reported twelve people present, not including herself." Pointing to one photo he said, "This cluster of people would be the family, I'd guess. She's managed close-ups of them, as well as those standing apart from the group." With a sympathetic glance at Carstairs he added, "You're not happy about this, are you . . . Intuition troubling you again?"

"Yes, damn it," growled Carstairs, "and I don't know why, except that I should have wondered why earlier. I've been careless—that coup in Africa, and Bartlett still missing, has been a complete distraction." He was silent, his eyes searching the unreadable faces in the photographs and wanting very much to know why they were of interest to Farrell. He said absently, "I don't recall Farrell ever asking for help before, do you, Bishop?"

Bishop shook his head. "To the best of my recollection, never."

"Exactly," Carstairs said, and nodding he said crisply, "All right . . . Top priority, Bishop. I want someone at Kennedy airport tonight, gate thirty-three, with passport and luggage. Henry Guise is free, isn't he? Give him a description of Emily Reed-Pollifax—that red-feathered hat should help—and emphasize that she and Rossiter are to be kept under surveillance every minute they're in Sicily, and if for any reason the two separate he's to stick with Mrs. Pollifax. Mornajay Upstairs will have my head for this if I'm wrong, but—"

"Better safe than sorry," said Bishop piously.

Carstairs gave him a reproachful glance. "Platitudes, Bishop? I also want to see the obituary on Estelle Blaise and any information available about her. Get on with it, will you?"

"Yes, sir," Bishop said, and hurried back into his office to set Carstairs' instructions in motion.

2

Monday

As the plane took off into the night from Kennedy airport Mrs. Pollifax had time to consider the last question she had asked of Bishop before departure. Actually it had been less a query than a complaint; she had said crossly, "Bishop, no one has explained to me how on earth you could find an agent to meet me in Palermo and travel with me to Erice at only a few hours' notice —I'm suspicious."

Meekly Bishop had said, "It's very easily explained, you know. Agents do occasionally take vacations and this one happened to be already in Sicily. Visiting an expatriate aunt, I believe."

So Rossiter had an aunt, she mused, and decided this was very promising, because if it was his vacation that was being interrupted he just might be happy to return to it once she'd connected with Farrell. *And I'll make sure he does,* she thought darkly, remembering Morocco, and the only other agent with whom she'd shared an assignment in which, because of him, she had very nearly lost her life. Definitely this Rossiter must be encouraged to return to his aunt, she decided; after all, two was company and three a crowd.

Putting aside these increasingly indignant thoughts she asked for a pillow and blanket from the stewardess, which she knew to be optimistic of her. It had always been a source of astonishment to Mrs. Pollifax that Cyrus could sleep so soundly on their travels by air. Considering the fact that no plane had ever been designed to accommodate a man of his size she thought his sleeping a small miracle, whereas she could only nap, wake up blurred and dull, nap again, and eventually resign herself to wakefulness. It was no different for her on this night: after being served dinner and reading a newspaper she briefly napped and was awake by midnight. Ignoring the film shown on the screen overhead she brought out the map of Sicily that Bishop had tucked into her purse, finding this of far more interest than the movie, which seemed full of dark alleys and murky figures being stabbed or shot. With the aid of a pocket flashlight she began a search for Palermo and Erice: Palermo was easy, being a major city and clearly defined on the coast but it took half an hour to find Erice, a small town in small print on the map, and a half an hour longer to translate kilometers into miles and discover that Erice was a drive of only a few hours from the Palermo airport. But in looking over the names of other towns on the map she could at last admit to a sense of relief at being met at the airport by someone more knowledgeable of the island than she, for how was it possible, she wondered, to distinguish between Petralia Sottana and Petralia Soprana, or Casteldaccia, Califimo, Castroreale, and Castellammare?

The film ended, breakfast was served—it was two in the morning by her watch and she set it ahead to eight o'clock. They landed in Milan, where she changed planes, and now at last she could look down on a marvelously blue sea. *Not* the Mediterranean she remembered from her map, but the Gulf of Palermo, and presently they were circling over land and beginning their descent into Sicily. Or Sicilia, she amended. Once landed, her anticipation overcame any drowsiness; she retrieved her luggage, made her way through Customs—it was all surprisingly casual—and walked out of the terminal building into brilliant sunshine.

She stood a moment, feasting on the brightness of sky and sun. Off to her right a fantastically surreal stone mountain rose out of the earth, beige in the morning light and veined with purple shadows. The parking lot across the road held a garden of small red, green, black and white cars. Standing next to a white car a man in a black suit, hands in his pockets, watched her. A young woman in faded jeans with a backpack and long braided hair leaned against a bright red car. A man and a boy stood waiting by the terminal's entrance, their eyes glued to the interior. The girl with the backpack left her car to stroll toward the building, but after a glance Mrs. Pollifax's gaze swerved to the man in the black suit who was also moving toward her.

"Mrs. Pollifax?"

Startled, she turned to find the young woman at her side. Automatically she said, "Yes?" and then, "Good heavens, you can't be—" She stared at the girl in astonishment, thinking her surely no more than college age: her blond braid was tied with a shoestring, her face sunburned and lightly freckled and her eyes a clear blue. "—can't be," she faltered, "the Rossiter I'm to meet?"

The girl responded politely but there was an edge to her voice. "You're shocked to find Rossiter a female? They didn't tell you?"

Mrs. Pollifax vigorously shook her head. "It's not that—it's your age. You don't look a day over eighteen and they said—they told me—"

"Yes?" she asked coolly.

"Told me I'd be met by someone very *experienced.*"

"Oh, *that.*" She sounded amused. Picking up Mrs. Pollifax's suitcase she said, "The red car is ours and I'm not eighteen, I'm twenty-six."

It was the freckles that did it, Mrs. Pollifax had to admit. As a child she had longed to have freckles, for what obscure reason she could no longer remember, and although Mrs. Pollifax might be startled to find that Rossiter was a young woman—and she was still *very* doubtful about her credentials as an experienced agent—nevertheless this Rossiter was a distinct improvement over the Rossiter she had envisioned; she was not about to be ungracious.

The girl unlocked the trunk of the car and deposited Mrs. Pollifax's suitcase in it. Opening the passenger door for her she said, "We ought to reach Erice by early afternoon."

"Not midday?"

"Midday is very flexible in this country," the girl said.

"You know Sicily well, then?"

Her voice was curt. "Yes."

"I think," pointed out Mrs. Pollifax gently, "that you can talk to me without betraying any secrets. After all, we're employed by the same people. I only asked if you know Sicily well."

She was given an appraising glance as the engine roared into life. "Am I being rude? I think it's that red-feathered hat you're wearing. Heaven only knows I'm accustomed to eccentrics—my aunt is certainly one—but you look as if you've just come from a Garden Club party."

Mrs. Pollifax said blandly, "Actually the Garden Club party took place two weeks ago and I wore a *blue* hat."

Pulling out of the parking area the girl gave her a quick glance. "I think you're trying to tell me something."

"Yes," agreed Mrs. Pollifax amiably. "And you're going to hit that dog up ahead if you're not careful."

The girl laughed. "All right, I'm called Kate, although really my name's Caterina, and you're Mrs. Pollifax?"

"Yes. Or Emily."

"I can't manage Emily yet," she told her frankly. "You look too formidable and proper. They told me *you* were experienced, too, but you don't look it."

"Exactly," said Mrs. Pollifax with a twinkle. "And you don't look twenty-six or—"

"Touché," said Kate ruefully. "You win. Now tell me about this man in Erice we're to meet, or rescue—"

"At midday," put in Mrs. Pollifax.

"I'm a fast driver. Tell me, will you recognize him? What's he doing here? Who is he?"

"His name is John Sebastian Farrell," said Mrs. Pollifax, "and he's obviously in trouble, or in hiding, and yes I'll recognize him, but I've no idea what he's doing in Erice. I know only that he sent an SOS asking for me and my husband—who couldn't come—and when we find him you can decide for yourself who he is. Aren't we driving very fast?"

"I told you, I'm a fast driver. It'll be slower going once we leave the autostrada."

"I see," said Mrs. Pollifax and thought it best to remove her gaze from the road and spare her nerves. They were close to the sea now, the autostrada lined with flowering acacia under a cloudless blue sky, and here and there she caught tantalizing glimpses of red and yellow flowers. To her left, in the distance, rose violent and volcanic shapes of rock; in the foreground she saw a calm mountain range, sharp stony peaks and closer wooded hills and rocky protuberances. The Sicilian coast appeared to be the only flat area on the island.

"Lovely flowers here," she murmured.

"In spring, yes," contributed Kate. "By August it's mostly brown, which is why I come in spring."

"To visit your aunt."

She nodded. "A bit of luck for the Department, I suppose, my already being here."

They flashed through a dark tunnel and out onto a flat and sunny plain, and Kate pointed. "You can see Erice from here. Or Monte San Giuliano, as the mountain's called."

"Good heavens," gasped Mrs. Pollifax, staring. "A road goes up there? The mountain looks practically vertical!"

"You'll see," promised Kate.

As the miles diminished and they left the sea behind them a cluster of roofs became visible on the mountain's peak, reassuring Mrs. Pollifax that people really lived there.

Presently, veering north, they arrived at its base to begin their ascent. It was a narrow road full of hairpin turns, with deep forests of pine on either side; around and around they drove until, nearing the summit, Mrs. Pollifax wondered how on earth Farrell had ever come to this of all places; she felt a stirring of very real pleasure at seeing him again and at learning why. They drove past a low stone wall lined with brilliant yellow flowers and arrived at a paved parking area suspended over the valley below; it was occupied by a tour bus and by four cars: green, black, brown and gray.

"We stop here," said Kate. "No public traffic allowed, the streets are too narrow."

Mrs. Pollifax, stepping out of the car, found herself staring several thousand feet down into what must surely be half of Sicily. It was breathtaking. Lifting her gaze she looked out on serried rows of mountains diminishing into the far distance, while below her the village and country houses clutched the mountainsides and overflowed into each valley. Beyond lay the sea, dotted with islands, while at her feet the shape of a city seemed oddly out of place. With an effort she returned to Kate, who was opening the trunk to retrieve her backpack. Glancing at her wristwatch Mrs. Pollifax saw that if the day was only beginning in New York it was half-past one in the afternoon in Sicily. "We made good time."

"Two and a half hours," Kate said triumphantly. "Now for the public square. I know the way."

They walked quickly down narrow cobblestoned streets lined with narrow gray stone houses; sometimes a door stood open and Mrs. Pollifax could see a courtyard with tubs of bright flowers and steps leading to inner doors and courtyards; they passed a line of shops selling Pinocchio puppets, souvenirs and pastries—"almost there," said Kate—and abruptly they arrived on a broad and cobbled square. It was a pleasing sight, full of space, and most pleasing of all there was an espresso café with chairs and tables set outside in the sun.

Kate slung her backpack over a chair and said, "What will you have? Espresso, cappuccino, a pastry?"

"Surprise me," Mrs. Pollifax told her.

Two young men occupied a table nearby, each of them affecting the style of French apaches in their black trousers and black T-shirts with bright scarves twisted around their throats. After one quick glance, as they gestured and argued in another language, Mrs. Pollifax turned to enjoying the pure luxury of sunshine. The air was clear and fragrant, and slowly she felt herself relaxing, touched by the peacefulness of her surroundings. The tall stone houses lining the square had an austerity that pleased her, their gray stone facades matching the ancient rough stones under her feet, the color happily relieved by bright flowers in pots on doorsteps. She watched a very erect man in a black suit emerge from the narrow street by which they'd entered the square: his chin boasted a wiry salt-and-pepper beard and he vigorously swung a cane that he dropped across a table not far from her, after which he unfurled a newspaper and disappeared behind it. Across the square a young couple wandered out of one of the lanes, both armed with cameras, and strolled over to take possession of another table.

Thinking it resembled a stage setting she turned her head with interest as another figure entered the square, this time off to her right, a solitary man limping badly. An artist, she decided, observing the paint-smeared trousers, the loose smock and huge-brimmed black felt hat shadowing his face, and then as he limped closer she began to smile. She would have preferred to leap out of her chair and hug him but just in time she remembered why she was here, and only drew out a chair for him.

"Farrell," she said warmly, beaming at him. "We meet again—under what circumstances I'm here to find out."

"Thank God you've come, Duchess," he said. "Where's Cyrus?"

"In Chicago."

"Oh God." He sank into a chair, pulled another one closer and propped his leg across it. "You have the photos? You have a car?"

"Yes to both. I not only have a car," she said gravely, "but Cyrus insisted I not come alone, so Carstairs found a companion who is capturing a cup of something for me. In there." She pointed, adding dryly, "We met only a few hours ago at the airport. That limp," she said casually, trying not to notice how exhausted he looked. "Have you been stabbed by a jealous lover, did you trip over the cobblestones or is it part of your disguise?"

"Actually a bullet," he said with a shrug. "It only grazed my ankle but carried away a bit of flesh as it whizzed past and it hurts like the devil."

She stared at him, really worried now. "It's come to that, Farrell? You really *are* in trouble!"

He managed a weak grin. "It pains me to say so, Duchess, but yes. I've been trapped on this damn mountain for two days and two nights, with a car I dare not use because they're watching for it, and as soon as I've caught my breath we've got to get out of here. *Fast.* You don't happen to have—" He stopped and looked up as Kate arrived at their table carrying a tray with three cups on it and a dish of pastries.

Kate said coolly, "I saw there were two of you so I brought a third coffee. You must be Farrell."

He stared at her blankly and then his

gaze fell on the pastries. *"Food,"* he said, and a second later half of an eclair was in his mouth. "Give me a minute for the coffee, can we take the food with us?"

"Farrell, what *is* it?" Mrs. Pollifax demanded.

He shivered in the sun. "I've been hiding in a dark storage room for those two days. A root cellar actually, I suppose. Food's the one thing I couldn't steal. Trousers, hat and smock no problem but except for three apples, no food."

Kate had perched on the edge of a chair to watch him. "In the car I've more nutritious food," she told him.

"Yes," said Mrs. Pollifax, "and should you be seen here in public? He limps," she added to Kate. "A bullet nicked his ankle."

"Bullet?" Kate said, frowning.

"Bullet," said Mrs. Pollifax. "Let's wrap up the pastries and go."

"Delighted." Farrell wiped crumbs from his mouth and then, accusingly, to Kate, "You're not Cyrus, who are you?"

"Kate Rossiter. Can you walk to the piazza?"

"Yes of course, but who—what—?"

"Later. Who she is," said Mrs. Pollifax, rising, "is not as important as finding out how on earth the pursuit of Julius Caesar's signature brought you to Erice to hide in a root cellar. For that we need privacy; people are looking."

"Yes," said Farrell, and unpropping his leg he stood up, promptly wincing. "Okay, let's go."

Kate Rossiter looked amused. Certainly there was nothing swashbuckling about Farrell at the moment, thought Mrs. Pollifax; his usual tan had been replaced by pallor, he needed a shave, his condition was that of a man who had been living on the edge, and she wondered if his ankle could possibly have become infected to further deplete him.

They walked slowly back through the cobbled lanes, with Farrell between them keeping his head down and trying not to limp. With infinite relief Mrs. Pollifax saw the parking area ahead and pointed it out to him. Kate hurried ahead to unlock the red Fiat; she held the door open and Farrell slumped into the rear seat, and then to the floor.

"Not to alarm you," he said, "but the whole point is not to be seen. I got chased here, that little brown car parked down the line is what I came in, and they know it."

"*Who* chased you here?" demanded Mrs. Pollifax.

"That's my problem, I don't know," he said, gazing up at her from the floor. "It was night, I was opening a safe in a villa that Ambrose Vica had assured me was unoccupied . . . don't know whether they were in the house or followed me there, all I know was I snatched up what I could from the safe—hearing someone behind me in the dark—and I ran. That's when I got hit—they shot at me—and once in my car they followed me. I don't know who they are or what they look like, I don't even know whether they saw me clearly, or already knew me, but they're *very* familiar with my car, having taken potshots at me while following me all the way up this mountain. And they were *very* serious with those guns."

"But what is it they want?" faltered Mrs. Pollifax. "What is it you found in the safe, for instance?"

He said miserably, "I don't know that either, damn it, and I had plenty of time to look everything over in my root cellar: a pile of papers and documents, but all in Italian. There was light enough in my hiding place to see that none of them related to Julius Caesar, though." He said darkly, "It would have to be—well, something else."

Kate, starting the car, reached into the glove compartment and handed Mrs. Pollifax a banana to give Farrell. She said, "But to hide in Erice of all places?"

"I know, I know," he complained from his crouch on the floor. "I've never been in Sicily before, it was night, I got lost, I took all the wrong turns, anything to lose them— except I couldn't—and ended up stranded and trapped on the top of this mountain, not daring to go near my car, which they've probably been watching."

As Kate backed out and turned, Mrs. Pollifax said to her softly, "Have you noticed? Those two apache-looking young men in black are leaving, too . . . the green Fiat."

Kate nodded. "Sitting at the table near us, yes."

Over her shoulder Mrs. Pollifax called to Farrell, "There's one thing you left out. If you could finally get to a telephone to send a cable to Carstairs during the night—"

"Credit card," he muttered. "Found a public phone."

"—then I'm curious as to why you didn't send out an SOS to Ambrose Vica when you're working for him, aren't you?"

From the rear he said angrily, "Because, damn it, I don't know whether I stumbled into a setup or not. Obviously *someone* knew exactly where I'd be, and exactly when."

"And Vica knew?"

"Of course he knew. He personally drove me past the villa the day before. Showed me where, told me how and when, and that everyone inside would be *out.*"

"I get the message," Mrs. Pollifax said. "Eat your banana." Noticing the speed with which Kate was negotiating their exit she said, "Kate, take it easy."

Kate shook her head. "The two apaches, as you call them, are behind us. So is a gray car. *Don't look.*"

Startled, she said, "Who's in the gray one?"

"Can't see. A man, I think. Hang on, both

of you," she called cheerfully, taking a curve at something that felt like seventy miles an hour.

Mrs. Pollifax braced herself for the next curve and as they approached it she glanced back once at the road behind them and was dismayed to see the green car keeping pace with them, and close behind. "Still there," she murmured to Kate.

"Yes, and so is the gray car."

Mrs. Pollifax realized that she was experiencing an acute sense of shock, not only at the speed with which they were descending the mountain but at the speed with which events were overtaking her. A night without sleep, a time-change and the race across Sicily to Erice had not prepared her for so sudden a plunge into Farrell's precarious affairs. *Wake up, Emily,* she told herself, *you can adapt, adjust and catch your breath later.* In the meantime she was experiencing precisely how Farrell must have felt two nights earlier when he had been pursued with just such alacrity; it was not a comfortable feeling and on such a narrow road she could foresee no happy ending to this. Obviously Farrell had been waited for, and when he'd emerged from his hiding place he'd been seen.

"What do you think?" she asked Kate quietly.

She said with equal quietness, "Nothing will happen immediately, not until we're closer to Trapani—that's the city below us. The road widens there."

"But the gray car, too?"

"It's still behind us, and nobody goes this fast unless—" She did not finish, they were rounding still another curve with a squeal of tires, and from a contorted Farrell in the rear came a yelp of anguish.

"We're being followed," Mrs. Pollifax explained to him in a kind voice.

He shouted back, "I would never have guessed it, Duchess."

"They're slowing down now!" cried Kate with a glance into her rearview mirror. Swerving around another sharp turn she leaned with the curve and spoke into Mrs. Pollifax's ear. "Whether you've noticed it or not, they've now missed two places where they could have closed in on us and pushed us off the road."

"Maybe the gray car inhibits them; it may be full of tourists, not apaches."

"Careening seventy miles an hour down this mountain? Not on your life!"

Mrs. Pollifax considered this. "They may want Farrell by himself—alone."

"You mean no witnesses."

Mrs. Pollifax nodded. "They may just— well, allow us to keep going, to learn where we're taking Farrell."

"Where *are* we taking Mr. Farrell? Ask him! We'll soon meet Route 187 and I have to know where to head, to the east or into Trapani."

"Where?"

"I told you . . . Trapani, the city below us."

Leaning back Mrs. Pollifax called to him, "Where do we go, Farrell? Where do you *suggest* we go?"

"Anywhere but Ambrose Vica's," he shouted back above the squeal of tires on another curve. "I want a large, impersonal and brightly lighted hotel while I sort things out. You need a hotel too, don't you, Duchess? You and Whatshername?"

"We'll head for Palermo then," said Kate.

"Lots of hotels there to confuse them, whoever they are. And my name is Kate."

"Look—I see a highway through the trees," cried Mrs. Pollifax. "And cars—we're nearly down the mountain!"

Meeting Route 187 they slowed down to enter traffic, and as Kate accelerated again a black car parked at the intersection swung in behind them, cutting off the green Fiat, and—yes, the gray one, too, still following. This was very hopeful, thought Mrs. Pollifax, because the black car inserting itself between them and the others gave them a small chance of losing the apaches.

Kate, glancing into her rearview mirror, said, "Now that we've left the mountain I think it's time to—I think we've got to find out who and which—*hang on!*" Abruptly she veered off to the right and down an unpaved secondary road toward a cluster of buildings and parked cars. "A *tavola calda*," she said. "Loosely translated, a hot-table place—restaurant of sorts."

"Food?" called Farrell eagerly.

"Sorry," she called back to him, "I just want to see which car is following—"

She did not finish the sentence. Both she

and Mrs. Pollifax stared in astonishment as the black car followed them down the drive, the green Fiat behind it, and last of all the gray car. "My God, *three?*" gasped Kate.

"Get out of here—fast!" cried Mrs. Pollifax.

"Yes," gasped Kate, and gunning the car's engine she made a reckless U-turn, knocked off the taillight of a parked truck and sideswiped the gray car as they shot back onto the highway, nearly hitting a car traveling east. When Mrs. Pollifax looked back, the green car and the black car had again fallen into line behind them.

"We've lost the gray car," she announced.

"Only because I hit it," said Kate.

To Farrell, Mrs. Pollifax said crossly, "You might as well stop crouching and sit up now, they seem to know you're here, in fact a surprising number of people know you're here. *Why?*"

"Never mind that, my ankle's bleeding again, damn it," he told her. "How far are we to a hotel?"

Kate said calmly, "We'll try for the Excelsior Palace Hotel, and I don't think you should sit up and be seen, Mr. Farrell, you'd be a very tempting target."

Farrell said nastily, "I don't think I caught your name . . ." But he stayed where he was.

Castellammare . . . Trappeto . . . Partinico . . . Monreale . . . The sky was darkening and talk subsided; they rode in silence, oppressed and depressed by the two cars relentlessly following. Mrs. Pollifax offered to take a turn at driving but after one quick observant glance Kate said no, that she was obviously the only one of them sustained by eight hours of sleep the previous night. A second banana was given to Farrell, who could occasionally be heard singing bawdy songs to cheer his spirit, or possibly to annoy Kate, toward whom he seemed excessively hostile.

"We're not far now from Palermo," Kate said at last, and with a wave of her hand, "This is the Corso Calatafimi heading straight into the city, then we turn up the Via Maqueda, which turns into the Via della Libertà, and—*voilà!*—the hotel. We ought to be able to lose them in Palermo. There'll be a lot of cars and not many traffic lights.''

Unfortunately the apaches in the green Fiat had apparently thought of this, too. Dusk having arrived, and the traffic having thinned the Fiat suddenly accelerated, veered out of line and pulled ahead to drive beside them. It did not pass them but stayed abreast of them until—

"_Damn,_" said Kate as the Fiat nudged the side of their car gently, and then with a hard thrust pushed them relentlessly off the road. They had no choice but to stop; the Fiat pulled in ahead of them while the black car drew up at a distance behind them: they were neatly contained between the two.

I do not like this, thought Mrs. Pollifax grimly, but she noticed with approval that Kate turned off neither the motor nor the lights.

Farrell, lifting his head, said, "What on earth—"

"Down!" snapped Mrs. Pollifax. She wondered why she bothered to caution him when obviously they were now completely at the mercy of their pursuers. She moved slightly to accommodate Kate, who was leaning across her; with one hand Kate opened the glove compartment and drew out a gun. "Hold this a minute, will you?" she said. "Be careful, it's loaded."

"A 9 mm Smith & Wesson," murmured Mrs. Pollifax. "I can't think of anything I'd rather hold for a minute! However did you smuggle it into Sicily?"

"Didn't," Kate said briefly, and rolled down the window at her side. From her pocket she produced a leather glove, inserted her right hand into it and casually reached for the gun, which Mrs. Pollifax handed over with pleasure.

The door of the green Fiat opened and one of the young men in black climbed out, brightly illuminated by the beam of their headlights. Mrs. Pollifax waited, scarcely daring to breathe.

He approached them smiling pleasantly, but she saw that he had a gun, too; it was in his pocket, his right hand resting on its butt just like a gunfighter in a Western film, thought Mrs. Pollifax. The scene froze like a nightmare, their car lights spotlighting the man's hard tight face and the black leather jacket he wore now. Mrs. Pollifax thought, *He wants to kill Farrell, he really intends to kill him—or take him away and kill him, drag him out of the car to murder him, and he looks—oh God, as if he's done this many times before.*

Beside her Kate sat waiting, too, the window rolled down, a pleasant smile on her lips as if she expected to exchange courtesies with the man, or to be asked directions. As he neared them he brought the gun out of his pocket and the scene unfroze as Kate quickly leaned out of the window, targeted him and fired her Smith & Wesson. Hearing three shots Mrs. Pollifax closed her eyes and thought wildly, *Remember, he wanted to kill Farrell . . .* Opening her eyes she was greatly relieved to see that only the man's right hand been hit; it no longer held his gun and he was staring dazedly at the blood dripping from his wrist. The other two bullets had efficiently punctured the rear tires of the Fiat, which were slowly—with almost comical slowness—deflating.

Immediately Kate backed up the car, ramming the one behind them, accelerated and pulled out into the Corso Calatafimi.

She said flatly, "That does it. I'm sorry but Palermo's too dangerous, we keep going. No hotel would be safe, the only place for you now is my aunt's house."

3

Mrs. Pollifax had fallen asleep when she heard Kate say in an amused voice, "Wake up, you two, we're here."

With a start she opened her eyes to see that it was night and there were stars in the sky. The headlights of the car were trained on a massive wrought-iron gate with an ancient crusted bell hanging beside it on a chain. Her gaze broadened to encompass a high wall that ran to the left and right of the gate before disappearing into the darkness. She said confusedly, "Your aunt lives here? We're here where your aunt lives?"

Kate's glance was sympathetic. "Yes,

and I'm going to ring the bell, which is a very *loud* bell. I didn't want to startle you."

Behind her Farrell sat up and rubbed his eyes; she saw that he had at last taken over the rear seat and had lain down to sleep. She glanced behind him, half expecting to see a car, other houses or traffic but saw only an unpaved and rutted road slanting downward; apparently Kate's aunt lived on a hill. At a distance she could see the tiny scattered lights of a village or town, and beyond this an empty expanse that might be water. Perhaps the nightmare of being pursued was over and they were safe, she thought, but only time and whoever lived behind this gate would stifle her uneasiness. She wondered what Kate's aunt would think of her niece bringing her two battle-worn guests in the night.

"Where are we?" she asked.

"Not far from Cefalù," Kate told her. She climbed out of the car to ring the bell, which proved just as loud and startling as she had predicted.

When the echo was fading Mrs. Pollifax turned to Farrell. Before she had so ignobly fallen asleep she remembered the serious thinking that she'd done and she said now, quietly, "Farrell, there's more to this than Caesar's signature, there has to be. I mean, there's the funeral, and the photographs you asked to be taken, and those dreadful men after you; there *has* to be more."

"Oh yes," he said sleepily, and yawned. "Damn it yes, there's more."

"I thought so." She eyed him sympathetically. "Did you sleep at all in that root cellar?"

"Not much. There were spiders . . . it was cold, too. Food would be a treat," he said wistfully. "I feel quite cross. I suppose I've been rather hard on that frighteningly efficient young woman who carries a gun and actually shoots it?"

"Yes, and if she hadn't," she reminded him, "you would have been carried off by that man, or—even worse—shot on the spot."

He groaned. "God, I hate being grateful to such a superior and wholesome wench scarcely out of her teens."

"On the contrary," said Mrs. Pollifax tartly, "she's twenty-six, she's CIA and well trained, is obviously resourceful, not to mention attractive, and what you're really saying is that she isn't impressed at all by you."

He had the grace to grin at this, his teeth very white in the dim light. "Right as usual, Duchess. Amazing how the ego requires nourishment once a man reaches forty."

The gate had opened a few feet and Kate was speaking to a swarthy middle-aged man in a white shirt; they both laughed and as she returned to the car he swung both gates open and gestured them inside. Kate drove through and stopped. "This is Peppino, we'll give him a lift." They waited while he closed and barred the gates and climbed into the rear, smiling at Farrell, who made room for him with a suspicious glance.

Looking ahead Mrs. Pollifax saw a long rectangular shape blacker than the dark sky: a sprawling country farmhouse from the look of it. As the car swept up the drive the beam of its headlights picked out a grove of olive trees on the left; continuing past both grove and house they turned into a drive at the rear and passed a magnificent garden of flowers that immediately pleased

Mrs. Pollifax. Whoever lived here, she decided, had heart. The car came to a stop and a door in the rear of the house opened to cut a sharp rectangle of golden light out of the darkness.

Kate, picking up her backpack, said, "Welcome to Villa Franca."

Stepping out of the car Mrs. Pollifax saw that a most startling woman had arrived in the doorway and she thought, *Her hair simply can't be orange, it has to be a trick of light, it has to be,* but as she approached the doorway the hair remained orange and grew steadily brighter. The woman was neither short nor tall, certainly not young, and it was impossible to find her figure because it was draped in a number of shawls over a long skirt. Her feet were bare. As she stepped back into the light Mrs. Pollifax looked into her face and was even more startled: bright mascara had been dabbed on each eyelid with careless abandon and her eyes were outlined in kohl. *She can't be a day younger than fifty,* thought Mrs. Pollifax, and was thoroughly awed by such an extravagant appearance.

"Franca, we're in trouble," Kate said very

simply to the woman in the doorway. "I've brought you guests."

With an interested glance at Mrs. Pollifax and at Farrell the woman nodded. "Of course, dear," she said, and to Peppino, "You'd better carry a gun tonight, Peppi, and be sure the gates are double-barred."

Farrell stared at her in astonishment. "Guns? Gates?" he muttered. "She's used to this sort of thing?"

Kate turned to them with a smile. "I haven't introduced you . . . sorry! This is my aunt Franca Osborne, and, Franca, this is Mrs. Pollifax and Mr. Farrell."

"I can't think why we're crowded around the door like this," said her aunt in her rich throaty voice. "Do come in, you'd like some food, of course, everyone does. Igeia?" she called. *"Anonin!* People! Guests!"

She ushered them into a huge old country kitchen, its ceiling striped with beams from which hung stalks of herbs and ropes of peppers. There was a fireplace and two iron wood stoves but the room was dominated by the long wooden trestle table that occupied the center of the room and was well lighted by hanging lamps. The two visitors huddled by the door, but this time just inside it, while Franca looked them over. "No pajamas, no toothbrushes, I suppose . . . Igeia! Food, pajamas, toothbrushes, two beds . . . *anonin!*"

A thin little woman in black came bustling through the arched doorway to the kitchen. "I'm here, I'm here, Franca. The *pasta con le sarde?*"

"There should be enough, and some wine—the Etna Rosso—while I give rooms to them."

Mrs. Pollifax, seeing one of the lamps flicker, said in surprise, "But those are kerosene lamps!"

"Oh yes, we've no electricity here," Franca said briskly. "We have a generator but we run it only once a day. Come!"

Carrying candles and flashlights she led them down an endless brick-floored dark hallway past a line of closed doors, and Mrs. Pollifax thought, *We've walked into another world here—or another century.* She felt quite disoriented after their race down the mountain and their brush with a gunman, and what a rambling and mysterious house this was, she decided, and certainly much larger than it had looked from outside. Opening a door at last, Franca pointed at Mrs. Pollifax. "You," she said, handing her candle and flashlight, and opening the next door summoned Farrell. "You," she told him.

"And perhaps a bathroom?" inquired Farrell with hope. "There's plumbing?"

A door to a bathroom was opened down the hall. "Bring them back quickly to eat," she told Kate. "Igeia needs her sleep." To Farrell she added, "Your ankle is bleeding."

"Yes."

She nodded. "Peppino will see to the ankle after you've eaten."

Ten minutes later they were seated in the kitchen hungrily eating a casserole of pasta, sardines and pimentos flavored richly with herbs. After serving them Igeia had disappeared, and Kate's aunt had tactfully withdrawn, too. Farrell said in astonishment, "Your aunt doesn't ask any questions about us?"

Kate looked amused. "We've interrupted her work, she's a painter. An artist."

"She has orange hair," Farrell told her accusingly.

"Oh that . . . it's a wig," Kate said. "It amuses her, she buys platinum wigs and colors them. If she decides tomorrow is a purple day for her, she'll have purple hair tomorrow."

"How—how extraordinary," said Farrell weakly, and resumed eating.

"No electricity is extraordinary, too," said Mrs. Pollifax, staring fascinated at the hand pump at the sink and the pair of huge wood stoves. Reluctantly she thrust aside the mood this house had induced in her and groped for efficiency. "There's a great deal to talk about," she told Farrell sternly. "Are you going to telephone Ambrose Vica about your abandoning his car in Erice, not to mention being shot at, or—what *are* you going to do?"

Farrell made a face. "It's much pleasanter to think of food and a real bed to sleep in tonight, and Peppino with a gun outside, although why Franca felt at once that he should carry a gun is very puzzling."

Kate said vaguely, "Oh. Well. Yes, I suppose so."

"Yes, but it's time we *talk*," Mrs. Pollifax told him firmly. "You've admitted there's more to this than you originally mentioned. You said so while Kate was opening the gates, and after all—three cars chasing us! I'll trade you the photos taken at the funeral in Virginia if you show us what you stole—"

"Borrowed," said Farrell with dignity.

"—from the safe you were robbing."

"You've got it all wrong," Farrell told her indignantly. "I protested very firmly to Vica about rifling a safe, at which point he reminded me that he was paying me a *great* deal of money to find and authenticate the Caesar document that this man Raphael claims he has in his possession. And it was Raphael's villa where I was shot."

"But who *is* this Mr. Raphael?" she asked.

He shrugged. "Vica is not given to confidences but his butler was a shade more approachable and said that Raphael had arrived a year ago in a huge yacht, leased a villa and settled down in it, presumably with the Julius Caesar document that Ambrose wants for his collection. What Vica *did* tell me was that he wanted to stop all the cat-and-mouse dickering and learn whether Raphael really owned an authentic signature, the man was being very tiresome, he refused to let Vica inspect it and he was wasting a great deal of Vica's time. Not to mention his money," he said, adding simply, "He's paying me thousands more than I'd make in three months' time in my art gallery."

"Art gallery?" said Kate, startled.

He looked at her as if he'd forgotten her presence. "Yes, art gallery. In Mexico City."

"But there were *three* cars chasing us," pointed out Mrs. Pollifax. "There has to be something *more.*"

Farrell sighed. "Unfortunately yes—since four days ago. Something different and very disturbing. I don't *think* I'm losing my mind." He stopped. "But if I'm right—" He frowned. "Disturbing."

"The funeral," said Mrs. Pollifax, nodding.

Kate pushed a glass of wine toward Farrell and he gave her another startled glance. Sipping it he said, "I hope I'm *not* right but I have reason to believe—it's why I especially needed you and Cyrus."

"Why us especially?"

He sighed again heavily, and Mrs. Pollifax

saw how tired he was. "Because the two of you were with me, and only you can help identify the man I've seen here. In Sicily." With a wry smile he said, "This will need a trip down memory lane for you, Duchess, it needs remembering Zambia."

"Zambia!" she exclaimed, and smiled. "Where Cyrus and I first met, and where you were working with the freedom fighters—"

"Yes, and you were there on safari—"

She nodded. "Yes, because Carstairs and Bishop had intercepted a message that implied Aristotle was on the safari, too."

"Who's Aristotle?" asked Kate.

"A very professional and *very* experienced assassin," she said quickly. "The Department knew nothing of him except his code name of Aristotle."

Farrell nodded. "He'd racked up quite a record, at least five known assassinations in Europe, one in the United States and one in South America, a man so colorless—and always working alone—that nobody ever noticed him or his gun. He'd hit and simply vanish."

"Well, there were disguises," she pointed

out. "When he was about to shoot Zambia's president he was—" She stopped and frowned. "Farrell, why are we talking about this?"

"Because I think Aristotle's here in Sicily."

"Nonsense," she told him. "Aristotle's safely tucked away in prison in France, given a very *long* sentence. For life, wasn't it?"

"I know," said Farrell softly, "but four days ago, not long after my arrival here on the island, I could swear I was introduced to him. He had a wife with him, they were introduced to me as Mr. and Mrs. Davidson. Five feet five in height, a mustache now, eyes that struck me as very, very familiar. Piercing eyes—you can't disguise eyes, Duchess. There was one other detail: do you recall how you described the odd walk of the man on safari who turned out to be Aristotle?"

She looked at him in alarm. " 'A strut and a stutter.' "

He nodded. "That's why I asked for you and Cyrus. You both traveled with him on safari before you knew he was Aristotle, which is how you came to recognize his 'strut-with--a-stutter,' as you called it, after he'd completely changed his appearance."

"But Farrell," she said reasonably, "how can this man Davidson be Aristotle when Aristotle's in a French prison?"

"That's been my dilemma," Farrell said. "I keep telling myself Aristotle can't be in Sicily but at the same time I'm sure that he is, and I have to say," he added dryly, "that given the events of this evening—and how diligently men want to kill me—I'm inclined to think my instincts could be pretty damn sound. I've upset *someone,* and it can't be Julius Caesar. I testified briefly at Aristotle's trial, you know, and if he recognized me, too, four days ago—" He left the rest unsaid.

"Where did you meet this man?"

"At Ambrose Vica's villa."

"Oh-oh," said Mrs. Pollifax.

Farrell nodded. "Yes. He and his wife were just leaving Vica—they'd lunched with him—they were standing in the hall as I walked through the door. Vica introduced them and jovially explained that Mrs. Davidson was about to fly to the United States for the funeral of her mother in Virginia."

"At last the funeral," breathed Mrs. Pollifax.

"Exactly. So I waited politely, several feet away, studying the paintings on the wall while Vica wished this Mrs. Davidson a safe trip. I'm very good at eavesdropping and she was a talkative woman. The name of Blaise was overheard as they finished their farewells, as well as her destination, Reston, Virginia."

"So that's why the funeral and the photographs," said Mrs. Pollifax eagerly. "Aristotle can change his appearance like a chameleon, but if you have the wife's picture, taken just this last week at a funeral, and can match it with old photos . . . ?" She fumbled in her purse for the photographs.

He nodded. "It's something that could prove I'm not crazy."

"Or that you are," pointed out Kate with a grin. "I didn't realize assassins ever *had* wives."

Mrs. Pollifax handed her photos to Farrell, and glancing over them he said, "Here she is, this is the one." He drew out a pen

and circled her face and Kate and Mrs. Pollifax leaned across the table to look.

"I remember her," said Mrs. Pollifax. "A
small woman, sharp-featured, cried a lot."

"You keep referring to him as Aristotle,"
complained Kate, "but surely he has a *real*
name?"

"They finally discovered it, yes. It's
Bimms, Reshad Bimms."

"Bimms?" echoed Kate.

"Extraordinary, isn't it? All those killings
and his name is *Bimms.* Pakistani mother,
English father, age forty-three at time of
trial. Army-trained, expert at sharpshooting,
dishonorable discharge from Army for reasons unstated. His wife attended the trial
only once and then, it was said, she panicked at the publicity and photo-taking and
wasn't seen again. But there'll be at least
one picture of her in the newspaper files."

"Did you personally see her the day she
came to the trial?" asked Mrs. Pollifax.

He shook his head. "Only a quick
glimpse but I do remember the news photo
of her. She's my only hope, Duchess, considering how Aristotle—what did the papers
call him?"

"The Invisible Man, of course. What else?"

"Exactly. When you knocked that gun out of his hand, Duchess, he'd actually turned himself into a black man, hadn't he? With dye?"

She said slowly, "Yes, but what we're talking about here, Farrell, is a man who was given a long prison sentence in Europe, yet suddenly you say he's in Sicily. It's very hard to *believe.*"

"Of course it's hard to believe," he said crossly. "I keep telling myself it's impossible, do you have to sing the same anthem?"

Frowning, Kate said, "It should be easy to learn more if this man Davidson is acquainted with Ambrose Vica."

"For whom you're supposed to be authenticating a signature of Julius Caesar," Mrs. Pollifax reminded him.

"Interesting, isn't it?" said Farrell. "Especially when Aristotle is expert at bumping off heads of state and political nuisances for anybody with money, and Vica's reputed to be one of the wealthiest men in the world."

Frankly puzzled, Mrs. Pollifax decided it was time to return them to the practicalities of the present: she turned to Kate. "I was asleep when we arrived here, do you think we were followed to your aunt's house?"

Kate looked troubled. "I was able to lose the green Fiat in Palermo but when I turned up the hill to the villa—I just don't know. There was a car behind us at a distance, but of course it was too dark to see its color. I figured there would always be a car behind us at *some* distance, I had to take a chance."

They were silent, considering this, and then Mrs. Pollifax sighed. "If we put aside the distraction of Aristotle, Farrell—"

"—only at risk," he said.

"*If* we put aside Aristotle," she repeated firmly, "your sudden popularity could still have something to do with Julius Caesar, and what you were looking for in the safe. That's where you were first shot and followed, isn't it? Let's go back to it. You said you 'snatched what you could' from the safe. What did you take?"

"I don't *want* to put aside Aristotle," he

told her, "but if you insist—" He reached into the pockets of his voluminous smock and brought out a small framed daguerreo-type and a sheaf of papers that he dropped on the table. "This is as much as I could grab from Raphael's safe, at least I was told it was his house before I fled with bullets flying all around me."

Kate grinned. "You have quite a devel-oped sense of the dramatic."

"Impertinent child . . . it's hoped you read Italian because these papers are all in Italian. As for the daguerreotype"—he plucked the framed picture from the group —"it seems to be someone's relative, aged eight or nine, circa 1800."

Kate, scanning the top document, put it to one side. "I can only recognize words here and there but this one looks a legal will. And this one has the word *affittare*," she said, scowling over it, "which I believe means rent, so it's probably the lease on the house of—ah, signed Albert Raphael. But this—what would this be?" Her frown deepened. "A list of names or of places with a lot of numbers."

Mrs. Pollifax leaned over to study it. "Did your Mr. Vica happen to mention how Raphael comes by his wealth?" she asked of Farrell.

"Shipping and oil was all that he said . . . Another rich one."

Mrs. Pollifax picked up the sheet to examine it more closely. "I wonder what the numbers represent? Here's *Osepchuk,* for instance, followed by nine digits. A telephone number? But the word or name of *Schweinfurth* has twenty numbers following it, and *that* certainly can't be a phone number." She glanced up as Franca wandered into the kitchen to cut a slice from a loaf of bread.

Kate said, "Franca, look at this, will you? Do numbers like this mean anything to *you?"*

Farrell made a noise of protest and looked daggers at Kate but to no avail.

With her mouth full of bread Franca walked over to look at the sheet of paper. "Looks like code," she said and continued walking out of the room.

" 'Looks like code,' " mocked Farrell.

"What would she know about it? And how many colored wigs does she have, and why on earth does she wear them?"

"They please her," Kate said curtly. "She's never been exactly conventional, even in the States, and who cares?"

Farrell said stiffly, "I'm sure I don't, but you have to admit it's unusual."

Kate smiled. "Everything is unusual here." Seeing Mrs. Pollifax yawn and look at her watch she said, "Look, we've all had a long day, I think we should wait for morning to decide how to get you out of Sicily."

Farrell's jaw dropped. "Get me out of Sicily! Are you crazy?"

She said coolly, "Mr. Vica must have advanced you *some* of the money that brought you here."

"Money!" he said in astonishment. "You think I'm going to leave without finding Aristotle, as well as Julius Caesar's signature? Or who keeps trying to shoot me, and why?"

"That's all very well," she said hotly, "but what can you do? You can't just walk out of here, someone could be parked down the hill right now, waiting for you. I told you it's possible we were followed here."

He said scornfully, "You surprise me. The Duchess tells me that you're CIA, and I gained the impression that you think yourself competent, but if you can't stand the heat—?"

She flushed in anger. Half out of her chair she said, "If that's what you think— Oh, how dare you!"

"Stop it," cried Mrs. Pollifax. "What's wrong with the two of you? Don't you see that we've got to think what to *do?* Kate's rescued us, Farrell, and given us a place to hide until the coast is clear, and quarreling is *OUT.* There's Ambrose Vica, for instance: I assume it was his car that you abandoned in Erice, what do you plan about that? For all you know he may be waiting patiently for you to return from your safe-cracking adventure three nights ago. We really have to learn whether he's involved or perfectly innocent—you owe him that much, surely."

Farrell snorted. "Innocent when he sent me to an empty house that wasn't empty?"

She said flatly, "I may be old-fashioned but certain courtesies ought to be observed, such as a man being innocent until proven guilty."

Farrell said crossly, "If you feel that way, call him yourself tomorrow and tell him his car's in Erice."

Mercifully they were interrupted by Peppino, who walked into the kitchen carrying a tray with three kerosene lamps, bandages, and small jars of what looked to be ointment. He said, "Gino and Blasi are on guard, Caterina. I am to see to this man's wound, which Franca says is not good."

Mrs. Pollifax said wonderingly, "My goodness, how many men work for your aunt, Kate?"

"They work *with* her, not for her." Rising, Kate took one of the lamps and handed it to Mrs. Pollifax. "Let's sleep on all this, I'm sure we'll all be brilliant in the morning, possibly even *polite,*" she said with a dark glance at Farrell. "Come, I'll make sure you find your room again."

*   *   *

It was a very nice little room, thought Mrs. Pollifax: friendly and cheerful with white-washed stucco walls, two wooden chairs and a plain small table, and loveliest of all a bed with a pair of pajamas lying across it, and a toothbrush. Extinguishing the lamp she quickly undressed, climbed into bed and two minutes later was sound asleep.

4

Tuesday

Mrs. Pollifax woke to bright sunlight—she had neglected to draw the curtains across the window—and lay wondering for a moment where she was, and then, remembering, sat up and looked at her watch: it was only six o'clock. What had wakened her was the sound of men's voices outside, and leaving her bed she went to the window and peered out.

By daylight she could see more of the house than she'd glimpsed the night before, and she was surprised to see that an ell had been added in the rear, a rather inhospitable-looking addition, she thought, with no windows in their proper place but slits high up near the roof, on which several bubbles of glass implied skylights. From her window she could see the garden; beyond this the unpaved drive disappeared down the hill on which the Villa Franca stood and now she could see what had awakened her: a small parade of men were issuing in single file from the opposite end of the house, each one carrying a shovel; she counted seven of them before they disappeared down the hill.

A curious sight, she thought, seven men carrying shovels at six o'clock in the morning.

"Now where is the bathroom," she murmured, "to the right or to the left?" She felt that she could have slept another three or four hours but as a guest of Kate's aunt this struck her as inappropriate, and more to the point she wanted to learn how Farrell was this morning. Opening the door to the hall she discovered that her suitcase had been removed from the trunk of Kate's car and had been deposited there. She fell on it with enthusiasm and presently, washed and dressed, she set out to reconnoiter. If there should be coffee available she thought she might even manage some serious thinking about Farrell's insistence that he'd seen Aristotle, but in the light of day, and following six hours of deep sleep, this seemed curiously unreal and quite absurd.

Farrell's door was closed and so she continued down the hall toward the kitchen, passing a huge living room, too dark to have been noticed in the night and much too baroque for her taste. It held a collection of marble tables, fringed lamps, overstuffed sofas, an array of hunting rifles over the mantel above a line of gilt-framed photographs, as well as ferns drooping and dying near windows swathed in dusty velvet. It was a relief to reach the kitchen.

To her surprise Igiea was standing over the stove, and at the table sat Kate and her aunt Franca, as well as three men in work clothes who immediately rose and left at Mrs. Pollifax's appearance.

"Coffee?" said Kate's aunt cheerfully.

"Love some. How is Farrell?"

Kate shook her head. "Not so good. Peppino cleaned his wound last night and says it's infected. He's running a small temperature and Franca's sent for Norina."

"Doctor?" asked Mrs. Pollifax.

Kate grinned. "No, Norina is the resident witch."

"I beg your pardon?" said Mrs. Pollifax, startled.

"Witch," repeated Franca.

Mrs. Pollifax turned her attention to Franca and tried not to react to her appearance. This morning her hair was a very tender shade of green; she wore no makeup but long silver earrings instead, and a smock much like the one Farrell had appeared in, heavily daubed with paint. Without the distractions of kohl and mascara she looked a sturdy and practical woman, her piquant face weathered by time and sun and yet at the same time, despite this earthy quality, there was something intriguingly childlike about her that interested Mrs. Pollifax. "I see," she said, adding pleasantly, "Then I hope she's a very *good* witch." On a more practical note she said, "I think it might be wise that Farrell not heal *too* quickly or he'll be off in an hour or two, hunting down whoever shot him—or others," she added with a glance at Kate.

"And get himself killed. He should *rest* today."

Franca looked amused. "I will convey that message to Norina. Kate has explained to you that he's quite safe here? She has also"—her eyes had a twinkle in them—"explained to me that this Mr. Farrell is a very difficult man."

Mrs. Pollifax shook her head. "On the contrary, I've known Farrell for a long time, and once in *quite* desperate circumstances, and there's no braver, more gallant man in the world. Absolutely."

Franca gave her a curious glance. "I see. Yes. Well, that's very interesting but in the meantime this angry man is asleep, sound asleep."

"When he wakes up," said Kate, "I think we should take a much closer look at those papers he stole—"

"Borrowed," Mrs. Pollifax reminded her with a smile. "Yes, we must, we were tired last night, but since Farrell's still asleep I might point out that he suggested—under pressure—that I telephone Mr. Vica today and report his car abandoned in Erice. I have a much better idea, Kate, I think you and I should pay a personal call on this Mr. Vica this morning. I'd like to take his measure, especially if he's involved."

"Mr. Vica?" said Franca, frowning. "Ambrose Vica?"

Mrs. Pollifax nodded. "Yes, do you know him?"

Kate said eagerly, "It sounds a capital idea, and Mr. Farrell will of course be furious?"

Mrs. Pollifax smiled. "One has to remember that Farrell is not himself just now; he has a fever."

"We have become conspirators," Kate said with a grin.

"I *love* conspiracies," said her aunt.

"Yes, but does anyone know where Ambrose Vica lives?"

"Oh yes, Peppino told me," Kate said. "A splendid palazzo well worth seeing, and I must say that meeting Mr. Vica sounds a good investment to me."

Franca looked at her thoughtfully. "No, Caterina, not you. I am thinking for the sake of this man you brought here you should not personally go inside once you take Mrs. Pollifax to visit Mr. Vica . . . if he will see her. From what you told me yesterday this angry Mr. Farrell must stay hidden and safe for a few days, but think of the vacations you've spent here! People notice you. People notice *Americans.* Mr. Vica need only say, 'who was that girl?' and someone may tell him, 'oh, she visits her aunt near Cefalù at the Villa Franca.' "

"Damn," murmured Kate.

"Kate!"

"Well, I'll miss all the fun but as usual you're right. Shall we go, Mrs. Pollifax? We can pick up some food on the way." Plucking several clusters of grapes from the counter Kate led the way out into the early sunlight.

As they drove toward the front gate a young man lazily rose from a bench near the wall and Mrs. Pollifax noted that he carried a rifle. "Good heavens," she said, "there's a guard here, and at seven o'clock in the morning?"

"How perceptive of Franca," said Kate, and rolling down her window, "Nito—*buon giorno!*" A few animated words were exchanged before Nito unbarred and opened the heavy gates. "Nito says there's to be a guard at each of the gates for so long as your friend Farrell is here."

They made their exit and the gates swung shut behind them but Mrs. Pollifax, appreciative of such security, was puzzled. "I'm going to ask a very impertinent question, Kate. Last night your aunt's immediate reaction to our arrival—without a single question asked—was to tell Peppino to double-bar the gates and wear a gun. Nito guards the gate now with a rifle, and you carry a Smith & Wesson in your car. How is this?"

She laughed. "It's the way it is here, that's all. It's not America. To live out here in the country and to prosper is to invite trouble. In general, you see, people are afraid in Sicily to live in the countryside if they can afford not to. The big landowners are absentee landlords, they've always lived in the cities, and only occasionally visit their farms and estates. It's considered—well, a little dangerous to live in rural Sicily." She hesitated before adding, "The people here are very poor, you know, and you can't blame them for resenting conspicuous wealth and sometimes—well, it can be a vulnerable place to live."

"You mean robberies?"

Kate nodded. "Robbers, bandits—at times, yes—but Franca is determined to live at Villa Franca. She's beaten the odds with her own personal crusade of developing the village just down the hill. She shares owner-ship with the villagers, although for now—and for a good many years—she's really been subsidizing it."

"Subsidizing a whole village!" exclaimed Mrs. Pollifax.

"Yes, and it's been lovely seeing it change. It's quite a cooperative now, the people eat well, they work hard, they have purpose and because they respect her they protect her."

"But isn't it," began Mrs. Pollifax tact-fully, "or rather, doesn't it strike you as sounding—well, somewhat feudal?"

"But much of Sicily *is,*" said Kate. "That's what Franca's trying in her small way to change, and of course what counts most in the village is that she's a di As-saba."

"A what?"

Kate laughed. "She inherited the land and house from her grandfather, who was

born on these acres. When she heard the
property was hers she immediately re-
signed her job in New York—she was in advertising—and came here determined to
find a way to paint her pictures and stay.
That was fifteen years ago. She's not an
outsider, you see, she's accepted, being
part-Sicilian. Both her mother and mine
were di Assabas, even if they went to college in America and married Americans. It's
family that matters in Sicily."

Awed by this disclosure Mrs. Pollifax
said, "But it must take a *great* deal of
money to support a village! Her grandfather
left a fortune as well?"

Kate overlooked this and said with a
wave of her hand, "This is Termini Imerese
we're passing, there are some ruins there
but mostly it's known for its macaroni. Are
we being followed?"

"Followed? Oh," said Mrs. Pollifax, still
digesting the fact that Franca supported an
entire village. "No . . . Yes . . . I don't
know . . . I don't think so, but there's a
white car at a distance behind us."

Kate nodded. "Keep an eye on it, will
you?"

*   *   *

It was with triumph that they reached their destination; the white car had not, after all, been following them, and Peppino's directions had proven to be perfect. At eight o'clock—an impossible hour, thought Mrs. Pollifax, but Kate was resolute—they drove through the gates of the Vica estate and followed a curving driveway up to an imposing mansion, a square and rather plain stone building to which had been added lacework iron balconies and a facade of arches to conceal its original severity.

"Good luck," said Kate, leaning over to open the door for her.

"Let's just hope he's an early riser," Mrs. Pollifax told her, and walked up to what she hoped was the front entrance, grasped the bronze head of a lion on the door and pulled it. After several more tugs at the lion's mane the door opened to a grave-faced man in black. Mrs. Pollifax explained that she was representing Mr. Farrell, whom Mr. Vica knew, and that she wished to speak to Mr. Vica.

She was allowed just inside the door to wait in an enormous, high-ceilinged hall with a ceiling of glass and a floor of marble. It was impossible to be unimpressed, for the hall was filled with statues and hung with paintings and tapestries: she moved from a Braque to a charming Matisse and wondered if they were originals. She had just arrived at a Modigliani when distant doors opened, a young man in a business suit arrived breathlessly to say that he was Mr. Vica's secretary and what did she want.

Apparently the name of Farrell was not without interest and she was escorted through an immense drawing room to a glass-enclosed room in the rear. Here Mr. Vica was breakfasting at a small table in the greenhouse, surrounded by trees in tubs and a profusion of flowers.

He rose as she entered, napkin in hand, and each of them inspected the other with curiosity. Mrs. Pollifax's initial impression was that he looked like a thug in gentleman's clothes. He was short and square, with thin strands of very black hair—dyed, she guessed—artfully arranged across the forehead of a lined and sallow face. He was wearing black silk trousers, a velvet smoking jacket with a paisley silk cravat at his throat, and also—but she tried not to notice this—a pair of warm sheepskin bedroom slippers on his feet.

He said in perfect English, "I am told you have news of my guest Mr. Farrell, who appears to have disappeared completely?"

She nodded. "Yes. Your car had to be abandoned in Erice, he would like you to know this."

"Erice!" Vica's brows rose. He said smoothly, without expression, "And there is perhaps some reason why my guest cannot tell me this himself? And may I ask how you know this when it is I whom he should be telling? Who are you, and where is he?"

He was not inviting her to sit down and Mrs. Pollifax felt no interest in prolonging her visit under such circumstances. She said crisply, "He entered a certain house three nights ago, he said you would understand what he means, and he found it occupied by two men who fired shots at him; he escaped in the dark and was followed. Not knowing the country he ended up in Erice where it was necessary for him to remain for two days in hiding. Where he is now he prefers not to say. He feels that he may have stumbled into what he called a 'setup.' "

"Excuse me," said Vica, "this word 'setup'?"

She thought, _He knows its meaning very well,_ and inquired silkily if the word "trap" might be more familiar to him.

Vica studied her with narrowed eyes. "Since you seem to have Farrell's confidence one may ask if this means that he met with no success in carrying out the job he was sent to do?"

She decided it was wiser not to mention that Farrell's success was semi and quasi, and that he had removed some of the safe's contents. "There wasn't time," she told him. "He was interrupted."

"How tiresome," Vica said. "Still," he added with a shrug, "there can be no accusations or suspicions or complications if the job was bungled. How amusing, I have made no progress at all!" With a sigh, "A pity he couldn't come away with _something_ . . . yes, a great pity."

"Mr. Vica," she said coldly, "your guest Mr. Farrell was shot and he was wounded.

This doesn't concern you at all? He was working for you, wasn't he?"

"True," mused Vica, "but how tiresome that he doesn't trust me enough to tell me this himself . . . Of course, considering the circumstances . . ." He was thoughtful, and then sighed again heavily. "I do not understand how this happened. Please tell Mr. Farrell that when he is restored I would urge him to contact me." He added with a lift of an eyebrow, "You are leaving?"

"I'm tired of standing," she told him.

"Ah—I see. But it is very early," he pointed out politely, "and you have interrupted my breakfast, which is growing cold. I did not catch your name?"

She smiled at him. "No," she said and left Mr. Vica to his breakfast.

"Well?" said Kate when she climbed into the car.

"I glimpsed a Cezanne, saw a gorgeous Modigliani, a Matisse and a Braque, and I've met Ambrose Vica."

"Tremendous! And?"

"He was very careful not to pressure me about where Farrell could be found, so I think we can expect to be followed. He finds it 'tiresome' that Farrell doesn't trust him enough to have returned to him, and he pretended to not understand the word 'setup.' "

Kate nodded. "Devious. What does he look like?"

"His appearance is a shade above that of a common thug, but not quite that of a gangster, and he is very, very smooth. Ruthless too, I'm sure, and extremely rich."

"I think," said Kate as they drove away, "he sounds quite the villain. If the Mr. Raphael whom he sent Farrell to rob is his enemy then I think Mr. Raphael's of interest, too, don't you? Of course only Farrell knows where the man Raphael lives, but—" She broke off to say abruptly, "How much danger is Farrell in, do you think? On a scale, say, of one to ten?"

Mrs. Pollifax thought about this. She said slowly, "If it *should* be Aristotle who Farrell met—and that's a big 'if' because I still find it so difficult to believe—but if he *should* be here the question I would have to ask is: how could an assassin imprisoned under tight security in France suddenly turn up in Sicily? You notice I don't ask *why* he'd be here, although this is of great importance, but *how* he came to be here."

"With help," Kate said grimly. "Lots of it."

"Exactly, so until we learn who is determined to harm Farrell it's obvious that he remains in grave danger."

"He's certainly attractive," Kate admitted, and gave her a quick glance. "But there's you, too . . . From what's been said, you're even better known to Aristotle than Farrell."

"He doesn't know I'm here," pointed out Mrs. Pollifax quietly. *Yet,* she added silently.

"Damn," swore Kate. *"More* guns and shooting."

" 'More'?" asked Mrs. Pollifax, made curious by the passion in her voice. "If it's not too secret, and if I'm not prying, what were you doing before you came here on vacation?"

Without expression Kate said, "Technically this is a rest-leave, not a holiday. I was in Yugoslavia, stuck in Sarajevo during the bombings, the fighting between Serbs and Croats, you know." She shivered. "It was a bloodbath. Food and water running low, corpses in the streets—we had to hide for days in a cellar."

"Good heavens," said Mrs. Pollifax in dismay. "How did you get out?"

"Not easily. And once the Department learned I wasn't sleeping nights and had this tendency to cry at odd times they urged this rest-leave." She gave Mrs. Pollifax a smile as they stopped at an intersection. "You have to admit that Franca's farm is an excellent prescription for any insomniac. But this sudden request to help you sounded so easy and uncomplicated!"

Mrs. Pollifax sighed. "They so often sound like that—as I've discovered all too often myself! But how did you happen to become an agent, Kate?"

She laughed. "Oh that—it's what I *always* wanted to do. I was born very late to a father who had worked for Intelligence during World War II, back when it was the OSS, and for quite a while afterward, too. He didn't talk of it much but I knew, and I adored him, and it's what I grew up wanting for myself—*much* against his wishes, I can assure you! But a week before I graduated from college, and a month before he died, he very generously—like a gift!—made a few calls to Carstairs that led to a humble typing job in the Department. After a year of that I was promoted to mapwork and then trained for surveillance; they found I was good—and I was!—and finally I earned field work. Just what I wanted!''

Mrs. Pollifax smiled faintly. "What strange ambitions some of us have . . . and do you think your father would be proud of you now?''

Kate grinned. "Maybe he'd not admit it, because parents always want their daughters to be *safe,* but yes I think he'd be very pleased.''

"I think so, too," said Mrs. Pollifax. "And are you able to sleep again now?''

"Yes, beautifully, and haven't shed a tear since I arrived in Sicily.''

Mrs. Pollifax nodded, and regretfully returned to the present moment. "Then I should perhaps tell you now that a blue car has been consistently making the same turns that we have, and has been following us all through Palermo.''

"Blue!" cried Kate. "Where did *that* come from?'' At once she swerved across traffic and turned down a narrow lane just wide enough for their car; they bounced recklessly over cobblestones, under balconies hung with drying clothes and barely missed scraping the walls of tall, narrow stucco houses. "Lost them," she said triumphantly. "The blue car was too big for that street. Now let's head for the Villa Franca. Do you think the blue car belonged to Ambrose Vica?"

"What I think," said Mrs. Pollifax firmly, "is that the Villa Franca is the only sensible place for us today. We are much too popular when we emerge from it and we simply can't afford to be followed back to it."

Some thirty minutes later, without further incident, they turned off the highway and drove up the winding unpaved road to arrive again at the gates of the Villa Franca.

5

Kate and Mrs. Pollifax separated at the door, Kate heading off to look for her aunt while Mrs. Pollifax went in search of Farrell. She found him in the garden, and was startled by the picture of gloom he presented; he was slumped in a chair still wearing his bedraggled Erice smock, and seeing her he said in a depressed voice, "So you're back."

Observing the expression on his face she said tartly, "The sun is shining, the flowers are brilliant, your foot—albeit propped on a stool—has a very *small* bandage now, but you sound as if you've lost your last friend."

"I wish we'd gone to a hotel, I don't like

this place," he announced crossly. "What I have been sitting here pondering is not the loss of my last friend but the loss of my sanity, having clearly seen something in my room last night that I have been assured this morning was never there. I might also add that after you left, absolutely abandoning me, I was visited by a woman whom I'm told is a witch."

"How interesting," she murmured with a twinkle in her eye.

He nodded and removed his foot from the stool so that she could sit on it. "You won't believe what she applied to my ankle, I advise you to keep your distance because it smells dreadfully. It *looked* a mixture of mud, green things and manure."

"And a real witch!"

He nodded despondently. "But the accusation that I've been hallucinating worries me the more."

"I think," said Mrs. Pollifax briskly, "that you'd better tell me about *that.* You seem to have had some extraordinary experiences during the two hours we were gone."

"Nobody believed me," he pointed out darkly.

"I will."

He suddenly grinned. "Yes you would, bless you." Straightening, he said, "All right, I'll tell you. When I walked into my assigned bedroom last night, bearing my kerosene lamp like a vestal virgin, I spotted this incredibly old Hellenic vase on the shelf over the bureau, and I mean *old,* very worn, with a marvelous patina of age but its colors still splendid. I may not be an authority on pottery but I can recognize a museum piece when I see it. Before I could look at it closely Peppino came in to bandage my ankle. After he'd left I lay exhausted on the bed, staring at the vase and wishing I had the energy to get up and examine it . . . but I fell asleep."

Mrs. Pollifax nodded. "You were tired. Naturally."

"This morning when I woke up it was gone. It had been replaced," he said bitterly, "by a cheap, gaudy imitation, very touristy, the sort you buy in a souvenir shop. Same size, garish colors, no patina. Frankly I was indignant, I went looking for Franca and told her that I wanted the vase back, wanted to examine it, that it was lovely. With great sympathy she said there had been no such vase in my room and that my fever must have been playing tricks on me—but I tell you, Duchess, I saw it, it was *there.* I think there's something very odd about this place."

"Well, if it has a witch—"

"A witch I can accept," he snapped, "but *not* being told I didn't see what I saw."

"I wouldn't like that either," said Mrs. Pollifax, but thinking that it was unproductive to remain on the subject she tactfully changed it before he grew even more outraged. "How is your ankle?"

"Actually it no longer hurts," he admitted. "I hear you went off at dawn and paid a call on Ambrose Vica?"

"Yes," she said, and described her visit in detail.

"Sounds as if he put on a good act for you. Did Whatshername go with you?"

"Her name is Kate Rossiter," she reminded him gently, "and no, she waited for me in the car."

He nodded. "Actually I'm not sorry you met him. If he knows that I've not abandoned him, and what I ran into, this buys me time."

"For what?" she asked.

"To look for Mr. and Mrs. Davidson—or Aristotle—who was *not* a hallucination or a trick of fever, I can assure you. Duchess, we've got to talk," he said, leaning closer. "This Julius Caesar business is nothing compared with finding Aristotle before he kills any more people, not to mention *me*. I want to find him, I insist on finding him."

"Yes," she agreed, considering this thoughtfully. "I'm sure that if he's in Sicily he has every intention of not being found, so it will be rather like looking for a needle in a haystack, won't it? And yet—" She frowned. "I've decided against all logic to believe it was Aristotle you met. I don't understand how he can be here in Sicily and not safely tucked away in a French prison, but you knew him, too, and if you saw him then he must be here—at least until proven otherwise," she added. "Do you think he'd been staying with Ambrose Vica?"

Farrell scowled. "When we met he was just leaving, but of course he was about to drive his wife to the airport, so frankly I don't know. But he'd certainly lunched with Vica so they know each other. Vica could be hiding him somewhere—possibly in his house—because although I spent two nights there it's a big house."

"You still have a temperature," she reminded him, "and there's danger waiting out there, Farrell."

He nodded. "I know . . . I'm willing to invest some of this day in convalescing because I'm bloody tired of limping and I'll need all my wits about me, but I'll languish *only* until tonight, Duchess. Definitely I can't waste a night, the only reasonably safe season of the day for reconnoitering. You'll help?"

"Of course," she told him. "What do you plan to do?"

"I want two things," he said firmly. "I want to find that house again where I was shot, and take another crack at getting the Julius Caesar document—if it exists . . . I've been thinking about that, and about those two men waiting for me, not to mention their chasing me all the way to Erice. I frankly find it very mysterious. Like this house," he said. "Did you know the generator was humming all night here? I woke up once and heard it. Somewhere below us, probably in the cellar."

She shook her head. "I slept too soundly, at least until some men talking outside woke me at six, but I don't see anything mysterious about a generator."

"No? Well, it didn't run for *us,* we had to make do with candles."

"Yes, but why do you want to go back to the house where you were shot? It's reckless."

He grinned. "Because it's occurred to me at some point during my profound contemplations this morning that if I return to Ambrose Vica empty-handed I've no reason to stay in Sicily."

"He'd dismiss you?"

"He'd have every right to. However, if I can have a second try at that safe, and search Raphael's house and find the Caesar document—"

"Steal it, you mean?"

"—find the Caesar document," he repeated, ignoring her remark, "I could then establish myself at Ambrose Vica's estate for *weeks* while I do all the proper tests to learn if it's authentic: the inks, the paper—probably papyrus, not parchment—and so on. I'll insist that you come with me—you can be my aunt—and what better headquarters for mounting an efficient hunt for the so-called Davidsons?''

She smiled. ''The idea has appeal, but the house you burglarized may not be empty this time.''

''It wasn't empty *last* time,'' he pointed out, ''but on this visit I'll jolly well have a gun with me—and incidentally, have you noticed what a fortress this Villa Franca is, and how many guns there are in the place? That's mysterious, too.''

''Bandits,'' put in Mrs. Pollifax, and repeated what Kate had told her. ''I assume you'll need one or two accomplices in this burglary, such as myself and whatshername?'' There was a twinkle in her eye.

He said grudgingly, ''Well, she *does* know how to shoot straight; I daresay she could come along, it's her car after all.''

''And the second item on your list in this plan?''

''Oh, that's simplest of all. Top priority, we can do that tonight,'' he told her. ''I want to do some prowling around Vica's house in the dark and see if the Davidsons are hiding *there.* Or his wife. I know the layout, and Ambrose isn't into drawing curtains at night —or conserving electricity either."

"How nice that he has it. I brought sneakers," she said, nodding. "Anything more?"

He said sheepishly, "Well, my suitcase at Vica's is in a bedroom just off the balcony on the second floor, and I'm damned tired of this artist's smock. It's boring. It's also filthy. I thought I might bring back some clean clothes while we do the Peeping Tom bit."

"Tonight, then?" Seeing Franca emerge from the door of the kitchen she said in a low voice, "Here comes Franca, can you face her yet?"

"After being told I'm imagining things? Not without considerable hostility, no."

"I've been admiring your garden," Mrs. Pollifax called to her. "It's lovely and so fragrant."

Franca acknowledged the compliment by stopping. "Of course water's quite limited here," she said, "which is why we lean on wildflowers and herbs, as you can see. Except for the gladioli and the tomatoes."

"Of course . . . chamomile . . . calendula . . . borage . . . wild daisies . . ." Mrs. Pollifax smiled at her, feeling quite adjusted now to the green hair. "I'd like so much to see your other work—your paintings, you know—if it's not intrusive. I'm sure Farrell would, too."

Franca said in a startled voice, "Oh . . . Well, you see . . . that is . . . it's so precarious just now, and—" Her voice trailed away in a cloud of vagueness. "Would you like another chair? Someone seems to have removed one."

Mrs. Pollifax gravely assured her that sitting on a three-legged stool was comfortable.

Franca nodded. "I must get back to work."

"To your art," Farrell said. "Yes of course. Was that your line of work back in the States, too, before you came here?"

Franca looked amused. "I was in advertising, responsible for the Toasty-Cozy ads. Lunch at twelve," she called over her shoulder. With a smile for her guests she cut across the garden to the skylighted addition that was apparently her studio, and Mrs. Pollifax saw that the door to her studio had been locked because Franca drew a key from her pocket to unlock it. A moment later she was gone.

Mrs. Pollifax, feeling rather snubbed, said, "She seems very sensitive about her painting."

"Probably because it's bad. Bucolic scenes of Sicily, no doubt. Peasants working the soil, or paintings of those jolly little Sicilian carts they drive tourists around in Palermo."

"Don't be cynical," she told him. "Unless that grandfather left her a fortune Franca supports a whole village with her work, in which case it must be remarkably good. You should have insisted. After all, you own a gallery and sell paintings."

"Supports an entire village!" echoed Farrell. "You have to be kidding."

"That's what Kate said. It's at the bottom of the hill, just out of sight."

"Let's take a look," said Farrell. "I'm supposed to stay off my feet today but we can see it from up here, surely?"

They rose and walked to the road that swept around to the rear of the house, and strolling a few feet beyond it looked at what lay below. The hill was steep but its slope was gradual and to her surprise the houses began at its base. "It's so near!" she exclaimed. "But it's so—so shabby."

Farrell laughed. "You expected something American? Model homes, newly built with garages and paved driveways?"

A track led down the hill to the village, which looked more like a hamlet in size, and as if its buildings had existed here for centuries. It was composed of two long rows of attached stucco buildings, stained with age; the two rows faced each other across an unpaved lane where she could see a few small children playing, a large number of chickens pecking in the dirt and a dog asleep in the shade. Behind the houses lay fields greening in the May sun, but the grove of olive trees that ran down the hill to their left cut off the view on that side, except for a huge pond of water in the distance and a number of outbuildings behind the houses that looked too small to be barns. The only new construction in sight was a square, barracklike building between them and the village, with an iron bell hanging at its door, but whether this was a school, a church or a warehouse its purpose was not identifiable. Beyond the line of houses a high wall of stucco defined the boundaries of the land, with a closed wooden gate facing the village street.

"She doesn't support it very *well*," said Mrs. Pollifax. "Look at those houses! You'd think she could supply a few cans of paint."

Farrell glanced at her in surprise. "But this is a real working farm, Duchess, and a prosperous one. Franca is one smart manager."

It was Mrs. Pollifax's turn to look at him in surprise. "I'd forgotten, you farmed in Zambia when you were working with the freedom fighters."

"And you, dear Duchess, have never known any farms at all. Franca's spent her money where it *counts*," he said. "See that pond of water? That's a reservoir for storing rainwater for the dry season, and if you look closely there are cisterns behind every house, and water pipes running up to them. That outside wall's been repaired, too; I don't know how much acreage is involved but a wall like that must have cost a small fortune. Look at those roofs, too, they're not old . . . no leaks *there*." He pointed. "And those trees to the right of us, blocking our view, are lemon trees, and what's more there must be a tractor somewhere because I can see the marks of it where the wheat or sorghum's been planted."

"I apologize," Mrs. Pollifax said meekly.

"I'm very impressed—you should be, too. Chickens, wheat, olives, lemons—most of all that reservoir—and now *I'm* intrigued by the fortune Franca must have been left by her grandfather. Which reminds me," he said with a glance at his watch, "I want a shave before we leave, which means borrowing someone's razor."

"Which could take hours finding," said Mrs. Pollifax cheerfully as they strolled back to the house.

In the kitchen they found Igeia preparing lunch and Kate setting the table. "How's the ankle, Farrell?" she asked politely.

He looked at her with suspicion. "You're wearing a skirt this morning."

"Yes."

"We're going to reconnoiter Vica's house once it's dark and his lights are on, and see if Aristotle is there. And I need a razor to shave."

"After lunch," Kate told him. "Obviously you're feeling better, Norina's herbs always heal, she's wonderful."

"I'll feel better when night comes," growled Farrell. "The thought of sitting around and doing nothing all afternoon is enough to bring back a temperature."

"I don't suppose you play poker?" inquired Kate.

He said indignantly, "You don't suppose *what?* Try me. If, that is, you know how to play it."

Kate grinned. "I play it and I'm good at it, too."

"Show me."

"I'll do that," she said and walked over to one of the chests and drew from a drawer a pack of playing cards. "After lunch? After you've shaved?"

"The shave can wait," he told her. *"Immediately* after lunch."

* * *

Fortified by Igeia's homemade soup and bread, and realizing that war was again being declared between Farrell and Kate, Mrs. Pollifax escaped the kitchen to look for a book to read. Wandering into the living room she thought how much this overstuffed room would amuse Cyrus, and she wondered how he and Jimmy were progressing in Chicago, but Chicago seemed light-years away to her at this moment. From a bookcase she picked out a ragged book entitled *The History of Sicily,* which looked fat enough to cover all the foreigners who had occupied the island. If it looked rather dull she decided that it would prove a needed antidote for an excess of stimulation, and carried it off to her own room.

She was propped up on her bed and sorting out the line of kings who had once ruled Sicily when the door opened and Farrell stood there. He looked dazed.

"What is it?" she asked sharply. "I thought you were playing poker."

"I was." He said in a strangled voice, "I've been exploring this house and I've just learned how rich Franca's grandfather was. No wonder she can support a village! But this time I want a witness so nobody can say I've been hallucinating. Come!''

She rose, happy to leave King Roger for the moment, and followed him out of the room. ''Sssh,'' he whispered, putting a finger to his lips. ''This way.''

Peering up and down the long hallway to be sure they weren't seen, he led her to a room at the very end of the hall, and on the right. ''If people want to hide things they should use better locks,'' he said.

''Farrell, you broke open the door?''

He grinned. ''No, I still have the skeleton keys I used at Raphael's.'' Carefully he slid the door open and uneasily she followed him inside. Closing the door behind them he pointed. ''Look at that.''

The room was obviously an office, furnished with a desk and filing cabinets, but what dominated it was a painting that had been casually propped up on the desk. It was magnificent, with rich deep colors— *singing* colors, she thought in awe. It was a portrayal of Mary and the Christ Child, beautifully tender, the two figures posed against a blue sky in which exquisitely charming angels hovered over them.

Farrell said, "I think it's a Correggio—it has to be!"

"It's lovely," she breathed.

"It must also be worth a fortune," he said grimly. "If it's an authentic Correggio, *millions.*"

"You think it really is?"

He was staring at it in awe. "One can't be certain without X-raying it, of course. I shipped my equipment here but of course it's back at Vica's house. It's Correggio's style, though, it has his touch and his colors —just look at that color red—and it's certainly old. You notice the tiny cracks in the paint and the water stain in the corner? Touch of mold, too, at the base. Just see those fingers—what craftsmanship! Beautiful. And the folds of Mary's robe? Exquisite!"

"I don't know Correggio's work," she admitted.

Farrell narrowed his eyes. "I'd certainly like to know more about Franca's grandfather. I wonder . . . If he fought in the Second World War, for instance—with the Italian Army, of course—it could have been something like that. A hell of a lot of master-pieces disappeared during World War II, the Nazis sent hundreds of freight cars full of treasures back to Germany. Many have never been found. If some of them reached Italy, and he was in the Army—"

"You're excited," she said, watching him.

"You're damn right I'm excited. A Correggio here of all places!"

"But, Farrell," she said uneasily, "we certainly shouldn't be here. We're only guests, you know, and I really think we should get out of here now."

He wasn't hearing her, he remained transfixed.

"You're not forgetting Aristotle, are you?" she added.

He tore his glance from the painting and stared at her. "Aristotle? Aristotle?" With an effort he returned to the moment. "Sorry! But you did see this, I didn't imagine it, right? This is important."

"I've seen it," she told him gravely.

He nodded. "And, Duchess, between the two of us we absolutely *must* learn more from Kate about Franca's grandfather."

"I promise," said Mrs. Pollifax, and grasping his arm she pulled him away from the painting and out of the room, carefully locking the door behind them.

6

In Langley, Virginia, Carstairs had been occupied with innumerable conferences Upstairs that had proven vital during a sudden
hysteria of crises abroad, all of them happening at once. He was completely unpre-
pared for Bishop's entering his office on
Tuesday to say that Henry Guise was on
line three and Carstairs had jolly well better
listen to what he had to say.

Carstairs, baffled, said, "And who on
earth is Henry Guise?"

"Henry," said Bishop patiently, "is the
chap who reported at gate thirty-three Kennedy airport on Sunday with orders to keep

Mrs. Pollifax under surveillance at all times in Sicily.''

''Oh God yes,'' Carstairs said wearily. ''You're not trying to tell me—''

''The circumstances sound rather bizarre,'' Bishop said. ''I thought you'd better hear them for yourself.''

Carstairs punched line three and picked up his phone. ''Carstairs here, what's been happening, Guise?''

At the other end of the line a disgruntled voice said, ''What happened was competition, nothing having been mentioned of this Pollifax lady being so popular.''

''Popular?'' echoed Carstairs.

''Yes, sir, that's it exactly. She met the Rossiter woman all right, after which I followed them to a place called Erice up on a mountain. They met a man there with a limp, shabby clothes, large hat covering most of his face. After half an hour they took off in a red Fiat to leave Erice with—surprise—another car following them.''

''How do you know it was following them?'' asked Carstairs.

''At seventy miles an hour on hairpin curves I draw conclusions. We get to the bottom of the mountain and damned if another car doesn't fall in behind them to follow.''

Carstairs said patiently, "And how do you know this second car was interested in following them?''

"Because," said Guise, "the girl driving —this Rossiter girl—was smart enough to turn off the highway to lose 'em or to see who was who. Both cars turned off, all set to trap her. I followed. The girl saw the situation, did a U-turn to get back on the highway, and bashed the side of my car as she passed. Hit my left fender so hard it tore open the tire. Everybody else left, I was stuck.''

"So you've lost them." Carstairs' voice shed its weariness and turned crisp. "All right, who were these interested parties, could you see their faces, can you describe them?''

"Only in the first car, the green one. Two guys in black shirts, tough-looking hoodlums, youngish. Reckless. Didn't like the look of either.''

"And Mrs. Pollifax—" He didn't finish this, he was wondering what on earth Farrell had gotten into, and what might have happened to him and to Mrs. Pollifax and Kate Rossiter once Guise lost them.

"I've checked hotels in Palermo," Guise said. "No dice. That's where they were heading. Also," he added, "I know enough Italian to check obituaries. Nothing there either."

Obituaries, thought Carstairs. Alarmed as he was by the implications of that word he was aware that it triggered something in his memory that had been overlooked. He said sternly, *"Find them, Guise;* I can give you one lead, and it's the best we have. Write down the name of Ambrose Vica. He's a wealthy collector who's currently occupying his estate in Sicily, I'm not sure where—"

"Near Palermo," cut in Bishop.

"Right—near Palermo. *Someone* ought to know where he lives, and when you find it keep the place under surveillance. The man that Mrs. Pollifax met in Erice has been staying with this Ambrose Vica; you may very well find that Mrs. Pollifax and Rossiter are there now. Let's hope so."

"Okay, got it. V-i-c-a?"

"Yes. And ring back as soon as she's

found, will you? I don't like my people disappearing."

He hung up and swore. "Two cars following, as well as Guise?" He shook his head. "What in heaven's name has Farrell gotten into?"

"More to the point," said Bishop testily, "is what he's gotten Emily into. Those two hoodlums sound like gunmen to me. What about Rossiter's aunt?"

"We'll save that for later, you know the problems we had in reaching Rossiter. In any case, Guise said that Rossiter was driving the car, remember? Vica's is the more likely place—if they made it there."

"If," said Bishop gloomily.

Carstairs sat back in his chair, frowning. "Guise mentioned obituaries, Bishop, why does that—" He snapped his fingers. "The funeral! Those photographs Farrell asked us for, and the obituaries I asked *you* for. Why haven't I seen them?"

Bishop said patiently, "Because when I mentioned it to you in passing—I believe you were on your way to a conference Upstairs—you only looked at me blankly and hurried away. It's on my desk."

"It?" said Carstairs with a lift of a brow.
"There's only one, from her local paper."

"Get it."

"Yes, sir." A moment later he was back
to place the single news clipping on the
desk for Carstairs to read. There was no
photograph of the deceased, and the obituary was meager: Estelle Blaise, widow of
Marcus Blaise, appeared to have lived an
eventless life, leaving behind three children:
a son Marcus Jr., of Washington; two
daughters, Mary-Marinela Asquith of Reston, Virginia, Jane-Petulia Bimms of En-
gland, and two grandchildren.

"This doesn't mean a blasted thing to
me," complained Carstairs. "Apparently
Estelle Blaise was a homemaker, wife and
mother. Small social life. Three children."
He read it again and scowled. "There's
nothing here at all, except for her penchant
for giving the daughters perfectly ridiculous
names, and the fact that one of them lives
out of the country. What can Farrell have
been thinking of?"

"Shall I toss it then?"

Carstairs hesitated. "Yes . . . No—
wait." His scowl deepened. "Farrell has to

have had a reason for asking this of us, you'd better check the files and see if we've anything on Blaise, Asquith or Bimms.''

"Right, sir.'' Bishop left, and ten minutes later rushed back.

Carstairs, glancing up, said, "You look as if you've seen a ghost, Bishop. What's the matter?''

"Here's the ghost.'' Flinging a sheet of paper on Carstairs' desk he said breathlessly, "We have quite a dossier on Jane-Petulia, wife of Rashad Bimms.''

"*Rashad* Bimms?'' repeated Carstairs. "That has a familiar—Good God,'' he said in astonishment, *"Aristotle?"*

Bishop nodded. "That was a tough one, wasn't it? Took years finding him. Actually it needed Mrs. Pollifax to catch him and—'' He stopped and gaped at Carstairs. *"Farrell asked for Mrs. Pollifax and Cyrus*—and all three of them were in Zambia when Aristotle was arrested, in fact Mrs. Pollifax was the one who—but Aristotle's in prison!''

Carstairs, staring at the report, said thoughtfully, "Apparently Farrell doesn't think he's in prison. Get me Paris—the

Sûreté—on the double, Bishop. Ask for Bernard.''

"You bet," said Bishop and hurried back to his office.

While he waited for his call to Paris to be put through, Carstairs scanned the report on Rashad Bimms, only too familiar by now. Turning the page he found himself staring at a prison photograph of Rashad Bimms, and attached to this was a newspaper photo of his wife as she made her exit from the courtroom. Mrs. Bimms, surrounded by newsmen, had flung up a hand to conceal her face but a photographer had nevertheless caught her from an angle below her up-flung arm and her features were quite clear. Carstairs reached for the pictures taken at the funeral by Mrs. Pollifax two days ago, and placed them next to the news photo. A few years might have passed but only the hat worn by Mrs. Bimms was different: he found her easily in the group at the burial.

He sat back in his chair, stunned by the coincidence. It was certainly difficult to believe that Aristotle was out of prison; if he remembered correctly, Bimms had been given a sentence that would keep him safely in a cell until he was nearly one hundred, if he lived that long. Yet Farrell—in Sicily—had somehow known that Aristotle's wife was going to be at a funeral in Reston, Virginia, two days ago. He must have met her somewhere, and considering how little publicity Mrs. Bimms had been given at the trial, Farrell could only have known who she was if she had been accompanied by her husband.

He returned to the photo of Aristotle and studied the bland and expressionless face that nature had composed so there was nothing distinguishing about it at all. He was Everyman and No-Man . . . a cipher . . . the perfect screen for innumerable disguises.

He was thinking about this when his call came through from Bernard at the Sûreté, and he dispensed at once with formalities. "Bernard," he said, "I've only one question: is our old friend Aristotle, neé Rashad Bimms, still in prison over there?"

The reply was passionate, and so loud that Carstairs had to move the receiver a few inches from his ear, and when he hung up he was shaken. Bishop, hurrying back into the office, said, "I couldn't listen in, Mornajay needed the report on—" One look at Carstairs' face and he poured him a cup of coffee. "Here," he told him, "you look as if you could use this."

"I could use something even stronger," he said, and Carstairs began to quietly swear at officialdom, corruption and various other insanities of society, while Bishop patiently waited for him to exorcise his anger.

"Aristotle's escaped?" he said at last.

"Worse—he was pardoned," Carstairs told him. "Eight days ago."

"Pardoned! *Aristotle?*"

"Heads have rolled. At the Sûreté they're livid, incensed, furious, and the government's launched a hush-hush investigation, a very quiet one because it is *extremely* embarrassing for them, needless to say, as well as alarming. Bernard says that it looks like big money behind this, and incidentally —and ironically—the pardon was for good behavior. It's obvious to Bernard that what lies behind this fiasco is power, influence and bribes distributed here and there, all accomplished quietly until Bimms walked out a free man. They suspect a Middle Eastern influence is involved."

Bishop whistled softly. "Bad news."

"No, *alarming* news. I wish I'd known it before sending Mrs. Pollifax off to rescue Farrell. I wish I'd known this before Henry Guise called, because if Aristotle is in Sicily—" He looked again at the obituary. "But he has to be," he said in surprise. "It's absolutely obvious now that Farrell believes he's spotted him, or why would he have taken this means of making positive identification?"

Bishop said in a shocked voice, "That means he's been sitting on his suspicions for nearly a week, and I hope you're remembering those two cars following Farrell and Mrs. Pollifax and Kate Rossiter."

"I'm not forgetting, Bishop," he said grimly. "If they actually met—had any contact—the recognition between Farrell and Aristotle may very well have been mutual. He testified at his trial, didn't he? It certainly places the three of them in considerable danger."

"From Aristotle."

Carstairs shook his head. "I'm not think-

ing of Aristotle just now, he's important only
if he recognized Farrell and said so. I'm
thinking of whoever had the power and the
money to have Aristotle discharged from
prison, and—before all hell broke loose—
smuggled into Sicily. It has the stench of a
real conspiracy, Bishop. One man alone
could never have pulled it off . . . *Someone* has plans for Aristotle."

"Don't," begged his assistant. "It was so
damned restful seeing off Mrs. Pollifax this
time with only a dead Julius Caesar to hunt
down. What are you going to do?"

"For the moment, nothing," said Carstairs.

"Nothing!"

"What do you suggest?" asked Carstairs. "The three of them have disappeared, we've no idea where Aristotle and
his wife may be hiding in Sicily, and I can
assure you they'll not be presenting themselves in public if they're still there. Until
Henry Guise finds Mrs. Pollifax or we hear
from her—"

"But they can't *know* he's out of prison,
they're operating entirely on Farrell's unbelievable conjectures!" protested Bishop.

"This is *Department* business now, there has to be some way to— Damn it, they've no idea what they're up against!"

"I suspect by now they know," said Carstairs dryly. "If not, how do you suggest they be told, when we don't know where they are? If Guise succeeds in finding them—"

Bishop said angrily, "Yes, but Mrs. Pollifax—"

Carstairs sighed. "One must be philosophical about Mrs. Pollifax, Bishop. We sent her off to Bulgaria to deliver a few passports to the underground and she proceeded to arrange prison escapes and the arrest of a Bulgarian general. We sent her to Mexico City to bring back microfilmed information and she ended up in Albania. There comes a time, Bishop, when for pure survival one must be philosophical, and you ought to know this by now."

"But with two cars following them after Guise was sideswiped, we've got to find out what happened to them!"

"I repeat, Bishop, there's nothing we can do just now. We wait."

Bishop said accusingly, "You realize that

at this very moment Mrs. Pollifax may be cornered and desperate?''

Carstairs sighed. ''Even if, at this moment, she is cornered and desperate, yes. I know you're fond of her, Bishop; I am too, but she's not alone. Try for some perspective! Try to remember we're neither the Marines nor the Red Cross nor the Ladies Aid Society—and I think Mornajay has just walked into your office and is looking for you.''

''Blast Mornajay,'' muttered Bishop, and stalked angrily from the room.

7

"**A**re you sure no dogs?" whispered Mrs. Pollifax, primed for adventure in sneakers, dark slacks and shirt, with a kerchief tied over her hair.

Farrell had already disconnected the electronic alarm at the gate—"same type I have in my gallery," he'd explained—and with the aid of a rope ladder that Kate had contributed, Mrs. Pollifax and Farrell now stood uncertainly on the grounds of Ambrose Vica's estate. The car was parked down the road with Kate at the wheel, and she had promised to bring it up to the gate in thirty minutes.

"No dogs, I promise you," Farrell whispered. "Don't forget I lived here for three days. *No dogs.* Let's go, shall we?"

A warm day had turned into a cold evening but the air was fresh and Vica's lawns newly mowed, the fragrance of cut grass lingering in the night. It was dark, but the villa ahead of them was brightly lighted both upstairs and downstairs. *Electricity, how lovely,* thought Mrs. Pollifax, having watched Igeia pump up water at the kitchen sink in the Villa Franca. Cautiously they made their way toward the lights, past shrubs and trees and through a garden with a bubbling fountain. Reaching a point near the front entrance, Farrell stopped at the edge of the curving drive. Pointing to the row of lighted windows he said, "The main hall you know. A library's on the right side, the living room's to the left of the entrance. Let's try the library first."

Mrs. Pollifax nudged him and pointed.

"Mmmmm," he murmured, for through the lighted window of the library the silhouette of a man could be seen gesturing broadly as he talked with someone unseen. Half-crouching, Farrell led the way across the driveway and in among the arches to the window. Providentially the window was open a few inches, which Mrs. Pollifax noted with delight. A surreptitious glance told her that one man was Ambrose and that he was arguing with a very elegant man in a gray silk suit. With the window ajar it proved unnecessary to peer inside again; flattening themselves against the wall they could hear fragments of conversation as the men moved around the room.

The man who was not Ambrose Vica said, "I told you, I made it clear . . ."

". . . are ridiculous, your terms," Vica said in an annoyed voice. "I want to examine the document before I—"

". . . receiving bids from others, you know that, a very highly placed Saudi for one, as well as—"

". . . bring it out in the open, Raphael, be reasonable, I'll match any—"

Farrell said in a low voice, "We're seeing Raphael at last."

"But no Aristotle," Mrs. Pollifax whispered back to him.

"No," agreed Farrell, and gestured her away and back to the driveway. Taking refuge behind an acacia tree he said, "No Aristotle but I'm relieved to see what Raphael looks like. After all, it's his villa where I was shot."

"The man who owns the Julius Caesar note?"

"So he *says*. You saw him clearly?"

Mrs. Pollifax nodded. "Not quite six feet in height. Broad shoulders. Very tanned, clean-shaven, very black hair, high cheek-bones, thin lips, nationality puzzling. Very *sleek*."

"Not bad," Farrell said admiringly, "but have you ever seen such a smooth and expressionless face? Very tight skin, not a wrinkle on it . . . *nobody* could be born with such a poker face, I strongly suspect Mr. Raphael's had a recent face-lift." With a glance at his watch he added, "Let's separate now. That balcony looks negotiable, I'll climb up, check the upstairs windows and retrieve some of my clothes. You see if any other rooms on the ground floor are occupied. Remember, Aristotle has a mustache now, and is about ten or fifteen pounds heavier."

"Right," said Mrs. Pollifax crisply. "Meet back at the gate?"

He nodded. "In twenty minutes sharp."

She didn't linger to see what talents Farrell possessed in balcony climbing, since twenty minutes wasn't long and it was a very large house. Immediately embracing her role of Peeping Tom she began her rounds in earnest but some fifteen minutes later, after inspecting each lighted room through its windows, she had seen a great deal of tapestry, damask, gilt and Louis XV furniture, as well as a man cleaning silver in the dining room, and an aproned woman asleep in a chair in the kitchen, but no Aristotle or his wife. Her tour completed she stole across the driveway, prepared to begin her passage back to the gate, only to discover this to be more difficult than on their arrival because she was leaving the lighted house behind her to face dim vague shapes rising out of an unrelieved darkness.

Stumbling over flagstones at the edge of the garden she located the shape of a tree ahead of her, but in making a dash for it she fell over a large and leafy bush before she reached it. Once on her feet again she more cautiously approached the tree and clung to it, saw another tree rising out of the earth at a distance, and with her eyes growing more accustomed to the night she navigated her way to it without mishap. It was when she reached it and stopped that she heard a snap of twigs behind her, and turned to see a shadow quickly move behind the tree that she had just abandoned. She was being followed.

She thought, *Farrell?* But Farrell wouldn't be playing hide-and-seek with her; *not* Farrell, she concluded, and fought back a wave of atavistic panic at being stalked in the dark. At some distance ahead she could dimly make out a dark mass of artistically pruned hedges. Forcing herself to walk calmly she crossed the long sweep of greensward and entered this haven of dark shadow. Here she stopped, turned to look back, and was in time to see her pursuer emerge from behind his tree and start toward her. Definitely she was being followed, and she braced herself behind the hedge and waited.

It was a long wait, and even then she did not hear him, but suddenly his shadow loomed up in front of her; she had time only to see that her stalker was a man with a beard before she stepped forward and delivered a quick hard karate strike to the side of his neck. Without a sound he crumpled to the ground.

A moment later Farrell, passing the hedge, stopped and said, "What the devil!"

"He was following me," she said indignantly, pointing earthward. "It's too dark to see who he is but I think he has a beard."

Farrell knelt beside him, brought out a book of matches and struck one that briefly illuminated a face with a very wiry black beard. "Not Aristotle," he said, disappointed. "Out like a light, Duchess—good show!"

"But where did he come from?" she demanded. "He was stalking me, and why do I think I've seen him before? Light another match, Farrell."

He lit a second one and she nodded. "Definitely I've seen him before."

"Where?"

"I'm thinking," she told him, and concentrated. "Erice!" she gasped. "In the public square when I was watching for you and carefully inspecting everyone I saw. Did you notice him? He had a cane and he sat down at a table not far from me and began reading a newspaper."

Farrell said, "I remember a man reading a newspaper but his face was behind it."

"This is very puzzling," she mused. "See if he has any identification on him."

Farrell's teeth gleamed white in the darkness as he grinned. "Duchess, you're the most illegal, illicit member of any Garden Club that I've ever met." Searching the man's pockets he said, "Aha, I think I've found a passport." He stood up and fumbled for a match. "Hold it, will you? These paper matches light and go out in half a second."

"He's American," said Mrs. Pollifax after his first match briefly flared, and when Farrell lit another, "He's American and his name is Henry Guise."

"Not very helpful," grumbled Farrell. "Not if he's in on this, too, and was 'stalking you,' as you phrased it. He certainly can't be a guard working here, not with an American passport in his pocket. Give it over and I'll return it to him, and then let's get the hell out of here."

"Just—leave him?"

"He's still breathing, he'll be all right. A bit cold, but—" He stopped as the man at their feet stirred. "Definitely let's go, Duchess," he said, grasping her arm, "and incidentally did you see anyone suspicious on your tour of the house?"

"Only a man polishing silverware, and a woman—a cook, I imagine—asleep in the kitchen. What about you?"

"Nothing and nobody, but I saw some rare and handsome paintings," he added grimly. "I'd kill for several of them."

Mrs. Pollifax, having just rendered a man unconscious—and not without twinges of guilt—said sharply, "Don't say that."

"Only an expression. Would you prefer that I 'lusted' after them? Ah, here comes the car and Rossiter," he said.

"Kate," she reminded him.

"Look, I've progressed from whatshername to Rossiter, give me a break."

Exasperated, she said, "I've never seen you so hostile toward any woman so attractive."

The sweep of headlights as Kate stopped the car for them showed her the mockery in Farrell's glance. "Ah, but you see, Duchess," he said, "there are forces in men that no woman can understand. *Yes,* I am hostile." With this he held the car door open for her, then jumped into the rear and Kate drove them quickly away toward the lights of the city.

"And so much for that," announced Farrell. "Tomorrow night Raphael's house, and another try for Julius Caesar, may he rest in peace, and definitely we go armed to the teeth."

Mrs. Pollifax gave him a sympathetic glance but said nothing, and they headed in silence for the Villa Franca.

* * *

Peppino opened the gates to them. "The house is asleep," he told Kate, putting a finger to his lips. "Be silent, you are okay?"

"We're okay, Peppi," she told him, and drove the car up the curving drive to the rear, while behind them Peppino closed the gates and barred them. Once out of the car they tiptoed into the kitchen, where a solitary candle illuminated three flashlights waiting for them, and three cookies on a plate. It was past midnight; they did not speak but headed for their rooms, where

Mrs. Pollifax, much too stimulated for sleep, changed into her pajamas and brought out the book of Sicily's history, certain that it would guarantee sleep within fifteen minutes.

With a pillow propped behind her she trained her flashlight on the print and read, *Under Agathocles, the Sicilian power carried war into Punic Africa, though without ultimate success, and . . .*

Abruptly the door was flung open and Farrell stood there, his eyes blazing. "It's gone," he said in an outraged voice.

Startled, she said, "What's gone?"

He stepped inside to close the door behind him. "The Correggio," he said furiously. "I wanted to see it again but it's gone, absolutely *gone.* We did see it there, didn't we? I didn't imagine it? I mean, I keep seeing things here that nobody believes I've seen."

Poor Farrell, she thought, and nodded. "Definitely I saw it with you. We both saw it, Farrell, you didn't imagine it."

He nodded and went out, angrily slamming the door behind him.

8

Wednesday

The sound of a truck changing gears woke Mrs. Pollifax in the night and she sat up in her bed in alarm. *It must be two or three in the morning,* she thought, and pushing back her covers she went to the window to peer out. Since their arrival back from Ambrose Vica's house a moon had emerged from the clouds and in its silvery light she saw three men in overalls walk past the house and down the hill toward the village. They were followed a minute later by Peppino, carrying keys and a rifle, but he didn't head for the village, he turned in toward the ell of the house, and to Franca's studio, where a light was shining. He knocked, the door opened and Franca stood outlined against the light; they exchanged a few words, Franca nodded and Peppino retraced his steps, passing very near to Mrs. Pollifax's window. She stood back and when he was gone the dark country silence closed in around her again, silent except for a faint hum somewhere in the house. She looked at her watch: it was ten minutes past three in the morning.

Does nobody sleep? she wondered crossly, and then, *What were they all doing at this hour when Peppino warned us on our return that everyone was asleep?* There had been a truck, she was certain of it, and what a pity it was that her room didn't look out on the front drive and the gates so that she could have seen it, as well as heard it. A rifle and keys . . . Peppino must have opened the gates for someone. And a light in Franca's studio—an *electric* light? The vague humming sound that she heard must be the generator that Farrell had spoken of hearing the night before, but at three o'clock in the morning?

Climbing back into bed she thought drowsily, *I'll look for a truck tomorrow, I'll ask Farrell if he heard a truck too, I'll ask why nobody sleeps, in the morning I'll . . .* but on this note she fell asleep.

She woke at six, her appestat still set on New York time, and despairing of any more sleep she dressed. There had been a truck in the night, hadn't there? Remembering what she'd seen and heard she vowed to ask what crisis had occurred, except that of course Franca would still be sleeping after working so late in her studio.

When she entered the kitchen, however —which seemed to be the heart of this rambling old farmhouse—she found a lively Franca established at the long wooden table drinking coffee with Peppino. Astonished, Mrs. Pollifax thought, *I couldn't have dreamed it, but how can she look so fresh and awake when only three hours ago I saw her in her studio?* Her hair, she noticed— and Mrs. Pollifax tried not to stare—was a radiant blue this morning and her blouse and earrings matched.

"Good morning," said Franca cheerfully. "Peppino is a very *good* manager, we are going over the bills and he thinks we can save fifteen thousand lire on the fertilizer.

Not much, but"—she poured a cup of coffee for Mrs. Pollifax and handed it to her—"every lire counts. He tells me you returned late but without harm, which I am happy to hear."

"Yes," said Mrs. Pollifax.

"And slept well, too, I trust," added Franca.

Igeia swept into the kitchen, muttering words under her breath, and snatched a pan from the wall.

"Actually," said Mrs. Pollifax, "I was waked up in the night by the sound of a truck, and I heard people. I hope there was no emergency? It happened around three—" She stopped, seeing Franca look at Peppino in surprise.

"There was certainly no emergency. Did you and your wife have guests, Peppi?" she asked.

"Me?" he said gravely. "No, no, Franca, I sleep. *Guests?* No, Franca."

Taken aback by their utter sincerity Mrs. Pollifax looked at Peppino, searching his very Italian—no, Sicilian—face, brown and sun-weathered, clean-shaven, with a rather large nose and soft intelligent eyes set off by a head of thick curly black hair. Meeting her glance he smiled benevolently. "No trucks at Villa Franca. Tractor, *sì,* no truck."

Franca laughed. "I only wish we had one!"

Mrs. Pollifax gave her a polite and sympathetic smile and said nothing, but her thoughts were less forgiving. *They're both lying through their teeth,* she thought, *and how very foolish of them because now I am very interested in why they must tell such a lie.* She found it necessary to remind herself that Franca had accepted their intrusion without question, and was providing hospitality as well as sanctuary for them, but her curiosity had been aroused. Considering Franca's remarkable simplicity—except for the blue hair—it was rather like discovering fungus, thought Mrs. Pollifax, in one of her healthiest geranium plants.

Breakfast, said Igeia, was *frittata,* which turned out to be an omelette flavored with herbs, and tonight, Franca said, they could have baths because the generator would be turned on to heat the water in the tank.

Farrell, joining them in time to overhear

the last, said, "Now *there's* motivation for an early return tonight."

"You find it safe to go out again?" asked Franca doubtfully.

He was gazing spellbound at her blue hair; lowering his glance he said, "Oh yes, so long as I occupy the floor of the car. Your witch performed miracles, you know. Actually I feel we should leave well before dark. You wouldn't happen to have a pair of binoculars, would you, Franca?"

She rose and headed down the hall. *"Con permesso,"* murmured Peppino with a polite nod, and gathering up his papers he made his exit by the kitchen door. When Franca returned she was followed by Kate, who greeted them cheerfully while Franca said, "It's very old but it's Swiss and in excellent condition." She handed the binoculars to Farrell.

"Thanks," he said, "because I feel that we *must* have daylight to find the blasted place again. I remember a hill behind the house, we can watch who comes and goes and plan our approach. This time it's *I* who plan to be the Second Thief, damn it."

"The what?" said Mrs. Pollifax.

He grinned. "It's what heist men call the gunman who sits back and waits while the robbers carry out their plans—while they crack open the safe or the vault—after which he moves in on them and at gunpoint takes the loot. No risk, no police alarm after *him,* he's free and rich. I'm exaggerating, of course, but in a small way I figure that's what those two hoodlums had in mind: to let me open Raphael's safe, then make their move, and—but who knows? It's what we have to find out. Are you both game for this excursion?"

"Of course," said Kate.

Franca said, "It's best I not know your plans, please."

"Definitely a sneakers night again," said Mrs. Pollifax wisely.

Farrell turned to Franca. "Now I'd like to use your telephone, if I may. I've decided it's time to call my host and reassure him that I'm still alive and still hoping and planning to conclude our—uh—transaction. If he's amenable, the Duchess and I will leave you tomorrow."

"Oh, must you go?" said Franca.

"I have to mend my political fences," he

told her with a smile, "I've been absent too long."

"He pays well?"

"Oh, very."

Franca nodded. "Then you must go, yes."

"So if you'll tell me where your phone is—"

Franca looked at him blankly. "Phone? But we have no phone."

This, thought Mrs. Pollifax, was really going too far. "You must have one," she said. "If you have no phone than how was Kate notified about my arrival at the airport?"

Kate intervened, laughing. "Oh, that. I had left behind a fax number for reaching me through the post office down in Cefalù. A letter was faxed to the post office—it was night in Virginia but morning here—telling the postmaster that I would pay the cost of delivering the message to the Villa Franca. After it arrived I went down to the post office and put through a call to Virginia."

"The boy charged a ridiculous amount to bring it here," Franca said indignantly.

"Yes, but he was prompt, you know, and

he had to push his motorcycle all the way up our hill, and it's a long hill."

"*Dispattista,*" muttered Franca.

"But it's ridiculous, no phone," sputtered Farrell.

Franca shrugged. "If we could have a phone we could also have electricity. Like many Sicilians we are too deep in the countryside, they tell us the phone lines can go no further than the highway below us but what good would a phone do us at the bottom of the hill? Who would hear it ring? And the cost?" She shook her head. "Now I must go to work so you will excuse me, please."

Farrell shrugged as she left the room. "I'd better make my call on the way to Raphael's this afternoon."

Kate nodded. "Once you're sure that we're not being followed, please!"

Turning his gaze on her Farrell said, "I wouldn't mind a guided tour of your aunt's village sometime before I leave."

And here, thought Mrs. Pollifax, was her chance at last. She said cheerfully, "Farrell was very impressed. Franca's grandfather," she dared to ask, "was surely a man of wealth and left her a large inheritance?"

Kate laughed. "Francisco di Assaba? Him? Good heavens, no, he left only books . . . old books, ragged books . . ."

"Books!"

"Yes, he was a scholar, you see. Well, not always," she amended. "When he was young he was a lawyer but he soon gave that up." She sighed. "I suppose he thought his books of great value but when he died it turned out the books he'd collected and loved were old, yes, but not at all what anybody else collected or wanted."

Mrs. Pollifax said incredulously, "You mean he left only the property?"

Kate nodded. "And books, the house was crammed full of them. When Franca sold the lot they _did_ pay the death duties and the next year's taxes but that was all."

Mrs. Pollifax exchanged a puzzled glance with Farrell, who said lightly, "No antiques at all? No _paintings,_ no artifacts?"

"Nothing, and wasn't she brave?" said Kate. "Now what time shall we leave? I could pack a picnic lunch, or would you prefer that I beat you at poker again?"

"No—I'll beat *you* this time," he announced firmly. "Get out the cards and stop looking like the cat who swallowed the canary."

"A very large canary," she teased. "Six feet tall?"

Mrs. Pollifax left them to their feuding, which appeared to be growing more amiable now that Farrell's temperature had subsided and his ankle was healing. She would brush her teeth, she decided, while the bathroom was clear, and wait until Farrell was alone before bringing up Franca's blatant untruths or the grandfather's lack of fortune. Farrell might not be interested, now that he was ambulatory and determined to be—what had he called it, the Second Thief?—and of course Aristotle was of far greater importance, whereas she . . . how *did* she feel, she wondered, and admitted that although she could accept Farrell's certainty that he had seen Aristotle, she had to work very hard to do this. It went against all logic, she felt, a man so dangerous to society and banished to a secure prison in France, except that as soon as reason told her this she had to admit that she had far more faith in Farrell's veracity than in any distant prison, and that someone minded very much Farrell's being alive.

At this point she could only remind herself again that logic was not always relevant in the scheme of things, and was even less relevant in the unorthodox circles in which she was moving.

Really, she thought, *this kind of circular thinking is extremely tiring.*

As she walked down the hall toward her room she noticed a pale line of light striping the brick floor at the very end of the corridor and opposite the office that Farrell had entered with skeleton keys. A door had been left ajar, and—curious—she tiptoed down to look. Confronting it she gently nudged it open and was surprised to discover that she had found an entrance to Franca's studio inside the house: from where she stood she could identify the door into the garden that Franca kept locked, but except for a huge empty easel in one corner the room did not resemble a studio at all.

But this is a laboratory, she thought in astonishment as her gaze circled the room. A long counter of gleaming white Formica ran along one wall, and even from a distance it was possible to identify two of the objects on this counter: a microscope and a Bunsen burner. A line of shelves over the counter held books and small glass jars; in the middle of the room stood a mysterious machine over which a sheet had been carelessly tossed, and the far end of the room held a large white screen.

A very well-equipped lab, thought Mrs. Pollifax, completely baffled by what she saw, and one that must have cost a great deal of money as well.

Guiltily she backed away and withdrew from the room, closing the door behind her, to stand bemused for a moment as she tried to make sense of what she'd glimpsed.

So far as she could see, Franca was not a painter at all.

Then what, she wondered, *is she* doing *in there?*

The question kept repeating itself in her head: *yes it's none of my business but what is she doing in there?* Small glass jars with powder in them, a Bunsen burner . . .

Could she possibly be involved in drugs? *What was Franca producing in her studio?*

She had just reached the door to her bedroom when Franca emerged in a hurry from a room down the hall. Seeing Mrs. Pollifax she looked startled. "Oh—I thought you were outside!" Her glance slid past Mrs. Pollifax to the door at the end of the hall. She hesitated, frowned, then walked quickly past her and Mrs. Pollifax heard the door to the studio firmly close and the lock snap.

9

At half-past one they were ready to leave when Nito stopped in the doorway. "Maria told me there's a car parked down on the highway. She went looking for wild fennel, the car was there when she went down the hill and still there when she came back."

Mrs. Pollifax said quickly, "What color?"

"Black, with funny windows. No way to see inside."

"Oh damn," said Kate, "that *could* be the black car from two nights ago, we haven't seen a black one since, have we? Thanks, Nito."

"Sure—be careful," he said, and left.

"I don't like the sound of that," Farrell

said soberly. "Two nights ago is when you brought us here, and you said we weren't followed."

Kate said indignantly, "No, I said there was a car far behind us and I took a chance . . . All right," she added, "it was late, I was tired, and I didn't want to drive another five miles into Cefalù to lose it and then drive back, and the car was *far* behind us."

"Quite reasonable," said Mrs. Pollifax to forestall any tart rejoinder from Farrell. "We were *all* tired, in fact two of us were asleep and of no help to you at all. Anyway, we can't be sure anyone parked there is watching for us, it could be a tourist needing a rest stop."

Farrell said grimly, "Only one way to find out. Let's go!"

Kate dropped a last orange into a string bag and slung it over her shoulder; Mrs. Pollifax picked up her purse and followed to the car, where Farrell took his place on the floor. Nito was at the gate and opened it for them. They drove through it and down the hill, and this time there was no doubt that one of their surveillants had traced them to the Villa Franca: the black car was still

there, and as they turned left on the highway to Palermo it started up and swung in
behind them to follow at a discreet distance.

"So—they've found us," said Kate.

"Yes," said Mrs. Pollifax, nodding, "and I
can't help but wonder, Kate, where we'd be
now without you and your aunt and the
gates and guards of Villa Franca."

"Definitely missing and presumed dead,"
said Farrell from his crouched position on
the floor in the rear. "Can you lose them,
Rossiter?"

"In Palermo, yes, but until we played
poker you called me Kate. Once, anyway."

"That was before you beat the heck out
of me, winning two out of three games.
Duchess, can you see who's in the car behind us?"

"Only the silhouettes of two men," she
replied, "but *must* we lose them? Actually I
don't see why we *should* lose them, I'm developing a very keen interest in knowing
who they are . . . or which," she added.
"It's very tiresome having all these cars behind us at different times: green cars, gray

cars, black cars, blue cars . . . I'd like to see who's *in* them."

"For heaven's sake, Duchess, what are you suggesting?"

"They need sorting out," she told him. "For identity purposes. We seem of interest to so many!"

"Wasn't meeting those two apaches, as you called them, enough for you?"

She said impatiently, *"They* drove a green car, now it's a black car, and the two men silhouetted in the front seat don't at all have the shape of the apaches."

Kate said over her shoulder, "She could have a point there, you know, it really would be useful to see what they look like. Easier to lose them, too, if we stop where there are lots of people. On foot, I mean. Mingle in a crowd."

"Gunmen love crowds," pointed out Farrell sourly. "That, for instance, is how Aristotle shot people—mingling."

"You're being very negative," said Mrs. Pollifax. "To me it simply feels time to acquaint ourselves with who it is that wants to shoot you."

Farrell said testily, "Are you suggesting *losing* them or mingling?"

"Whatever it takes to see what they look like."

"The cathedral's a possibility," said Kate. "No one would dare any rough stuff in a cathedral and there are always tour guides and tourists there. We could join them, and once our two surveillants are tangled up in the crowd we can make a dash back to the car."

"I thought I was to stay hidden and not be seen," pointed out Farrell reproachfully. "And what if it's the Mafia behind all this? There's still a Mafia here, isn't there?"

"You mean the *onorata società,* which is what Sicilians call them? Lately they've only been killing each other," said Kate. "I don't think you'd still be alive if it was *them.*"

"Thanks so much," grumbled Farrell. "Of course it's only my life that's involved here, a meager thing at best, but it's mine. However, I suppose I'm outvoted?"

Kate said, "I vote yes with Mrs. Pollifax but I'll bring the gun in my purse."

"Madness," muttered Farrell.

Mrs. Pollifax was inclined to agree with

him; after all, it was he who was in danger and it was not at all pleasant to use him as bait. On the other hand it was now obvious that these people had traced them to the Villa Franca and she didn't think that Farrell had considered yet how vulnerable this made both them and the villa; they would have to leave the villa, of course, but still without any knowledge of who wanted him killed. She thought the events that had taken place since she'd met Farrell in Erice had been persistent enough to prove that someone with real power and money was orchestrating these attempts to curb Farrell. It was difficult to link them with any signature of Julius Caesar; if Aristotle was in Sicily and responsible for this violence then it needed a bold move to learn who was protecting him; they needed faces, license plate numbers and names, and this meant risk.

"The cathedral's ahead," said Kate, pointing.

She had been right about its being a populated area. A tour bus was discharging a bus full of passengers; the narrow street down which they drove was lined with

shops selling ceramics, mosaics and souvenirs, as well as tourists gazing in their
windows. On the right, a wide staircase led
down into a huge square rimmed with baroque buildings of yellow stone, one of
which bore a dome. Beside the steps,
marking the entrance into the square, stood
an ornate fountain.

Kate pointed to a parking space farther
down the street beyond the fountain. "I assume our surveillants don't know me, so I'll
drive on and park in that space, but you
hop out and join that group of tourists—
quickly now—and I'll catch up with you."

She stopped the car, Mrs. Pollifax
jumped out and opened the back door; Farrell reared up from his position on the floor,
stepped out, and the two of them tried not
to look conspicuous as they descended the
staircase to enter the cathedral piazza.

It was a lively scene: two colorful Sicilian
donkey carts stood waiting for customers, a
third was being driven away carrying a pair
of exuberant and waving tourists. Tables
had been set up here and there to sell
leather handbags, books and maps; a cos-
tumed photographer hovered over a cam-

era on a tripod waiting for prey; and at a distance a man in uniform was shepherding a group of tourists into the dome-topped cathedral. Stopping at the base of the staircase Mrs. Pollifax and Farrell joined the small crowd waiting uncertainly for their guide to empty his tour bus. It proved a long wait because it was necessary for the guide to help a woman on crutches down the stairs, and as he joined them at last, Kate arrived on the top step, glanced around, saw them and slowly walked down to join them.

"You don't seem in a hurry," growled Farrell.

"I'm giving them time," she explained brightly. "They parked several cars ahead of me and had the dickens of a time backing into the space. I didn't recognize either of them, by the way. One of them is wearing a hot-looking tweed jacket, the other has a bright green shirt."

"New talent," said Farrell gloomily.

She gave him an exasperated glance. "Shall we go? The entrance is over there and I see a new tour group starting out just inside the door."

"We begin the mingling now?" quipped Farrell.

"Loosen up," Kate said. "If it'll give you a sense of perspective this cathedral was completed seven centuries ago, about 1185, and even then it was built over an earlier church, a mosque."

"If that's to promote humility," Farrell told her, "it's only a reminder of how many kings got bumped off in those days . . . assassinated, if you're familiar with the word?"

"Sssh," hissed Kate as the guard began to speak.

". . . upon entering you will see that the interior is cross-shaped, with a nave and two aisles. Now if you will follow me, please, and proceed—yes, that's right—down this aisle, which contains the Tombs of the Kings . . ." The guide paused for his constituents to surround him, and Mrs. Pollifax reflected how guides all over the world seemed to speak in the same mellifluous and somewhat pompous manner.

He nodded at them now, pleased at their orderly assembly. "Ah yes," he began, "you will see here, lining this wall, the admirably executed sarcophagi of porphyry, surmounted by canopies . . . Here reposes the emperor Frederick II, who died in 1250, and to the right lies his father Henry VI, who died in 1197. Behind, to the left, is the tomb of King Roger, whose death occurred in 1154, and on the right, in the sarcophagus adorned with an eagle, rests his daughter Constance, wife of Henry VI. On the left—in that niche—lies the son of Frederick III of Aragon, and . . ."

Mrs. Pollifax sighed, rather overpowered by so many dates and kings, and finding nothing at all romantic about lists. Shifting her position she accidentally stepped on the foot of the woman beside her who recoiled, bumping into the man in front of her, who turned and gave Mrs. Pollifax's neighbor a scathing glance. Mrs. Pollifax found herself pushed forward while the two confronted each other, and then pushed aside to the front as the crowd adjusted itself to this minor disturbance.

"In 1781," the guide was complacently telling them, "the sarcophagi were transferred here from a chapel contiguous to the choir, and opened. The remains of Roger, Henry VI and Constance were greatly decomposed, while those of Frederick II were in good preservation. The corpse of the emperor . . ."

Mrs. Pollifax sighed, and removed her gaze from the guide to find herself looking directly into the eyes of a man who was staring at her with an astonishment that approached horror. He stood off to her right, at the edge of the group, and she knew those eyes: they had met hers with equal astonishment in a different country, and only seconds before he'd lifted a gun to kill her.

He really was here. In Sicily.

She thought, *I'd forgotten how small he is . . .* and then, *he's as shocked to see me as I am to see him, and now there are two of us he'll have to kill.*

She became aware that Farrell was touching her elbow. "Duchess?" he said in a low voice.

"Yes," she said, feeling a little sick, and turned to blindly push her way out of the crowd.

Kate stood on the periphery of the group, looking for them anxiously. Seeing Farrell she said, "You found her? Thank God— let's *go!*"

Even as they hurried toward the door Mrs. Pollifax found herself distrusting such instant recognition as she recalled the neatly trimmed mustache, the broader waist and the English tweeds he wore. *Only the eyes,* she thought, *the eyes . . .* and said aloud, "He should have worn dark glasses, he was a *fool* not to wear dark glasses, I could see his eyes."

"Who?" demanded Farrell.

"Aristotle."

He stopped to stare at her. "You saw him, too? You *recognized* him?"

"Don't stop," cried Kate, and as they reached the doorway, *"RUN!"*

Mrs. Pollifax ran. The open square lay before her and it looked a long way to the steps. Another tour group was arriving and Mrs. Pollifax kept her eyes on them, picturing herself safely among them and pacing herself by their growing nearness. She was not far from them when something very small and metallic whished past her ear, slicing the air to hit the pavement in front of her and to send up a cloud of dust, and splinters of concrete. *That was a bullet,* she thought in surprise, and a moment later reached the steps.

Farrell, catching up with her, gasped, "Damn it, he nearly hit you, Duchess. That was a *bullet,* are you all right?"

She did not trouble to answer, it was difficult enough to catch her breath. She saw that Kate had outpaced them both and was already at the door of the car and unlocking it. Mrs. Pollifax fell into the front seat, heard Farrell slam the door behind him, Kate backed up and headed out into the street.

Regaining her voice Mrs. Pollifax said, "Prison has certainly undermined Aristotle's marksmanship, he *missed* me."

"Barely," said Farrell, and tossed a spent bullet into her lap. "A little souvenir for you, I stopped and picked it up."

"That was reckless of you," she told him.

"What bullet?" demanded Kate, making a fast turn up a side street. "Will someone please tell me what's been happening? They shot at you, Farrell?"

"No, at the Duchess," he said grimly. "I was running at least fifteen feet off to the side of her, so it could only have been aimed at her. They're not following us, are they?"

"No," said Kate. "They'd not even left the cathedral square when we zoomed away."

"You saw Aristotle, Duchess, and I take it he saw you, too."

She nodded. "It was his staring at me that caught my eye."

"How did he look, seeing you?"

"As if he'd seen a ghost. Horrified."

"So now you're on his hit list, too," he said bitterly. "At which point he must have decided you were an easier target than I was."

"But he *missed,*" she said, frowning. "That's difficult to understand."

Kate, glancing at her in the rearview mirror, said, "Farrell, whether you've noticed it or not, Mrs. Pollifax looks very shaken-up. Enough talk of guns and Aristotle!"

Farrell gave Mrs. Pollifax a searching look. "Some brandy, maybe? We could stop somewhere—"

"I've a better idea," interrupted Kate. "I suggest a stop at Segesta on the way to Raphael's villa, it's my favorite place and if we take the inland route 113 we'd pass it anyway. It's lovely and peaceful: the ruins of a city with its streets grown over with grass, and an ancient theater and a view for miles around . . . just sky and wind!"

"Very poetic," murmured Farrell, "but you understand that finding Raphael's house, not to mention locating a surveillance point, is going to take time?"

"Understood," said Kate, "but I can't think of a more perfect antidote for Mrs. Pollifax to heal the shock of meeting Aristotle, and hearing a bullet whizz past her, and much kinder than brandy."

How very thoughtful of her, reflected Mrs. Pollifax, acknowledging that she felt unnerved, not so much by the bullet that Farrell had tossed into her lap but at the shock of actually seeing Aristotle again. "It sounds lovely," she said.

"Good—let's go," Farrell told her. "Time we saw something more of this island anyway, and, Duchess—sorry I wasn't more aware, I was busy gloating over Aristotle's missing you."

"Which I still find surprising."

"Well, they don't encourage practice shooting in prisons," he reminded her.

The highway was now a familiar one, and Mrs. Pollifax tried not to remember that on their return from Erice along this same route they had been closely followed and then forcibly stopped by the two apaches. Abruptly, as if she too was thinking of this, Kate said, "We turn here to bypass Partinico and go inland to Segesta. Incidentally, Partinico is where Danilo Dolci has done so much for the people, fighting the government and the mafiosos to build schools and cooperatives and a dam. A saint, believe me, and Franca's inspiration, of course. Up in the hills near here lived Sicily's famous bandit, Salvatore Giuliano. Folk hero or terrorist, take your pick."

"Still alive?"

"Oh no, murdered, no one's certain by whom. In 1950, I think."

They drove over low hills, under a tunnel and then through a town called Alcamo, and as the road descended, past pines and olive trees, Kate pointed. "Look, you can see in the distance the ruins at the top of Monte Bárbaro."

"Missed it," said Farrell.

"Clumsy," teased Kate.

They parked the car near the top of the mountain and began their walk up a gradually rising path to the theater ruins. They walked with a meadow at one side, bright with daisies, scarlet poppies, and here and there banks of brilliant yellow and purple flowers. A faint breeze stirred the grass and the tops of olive trees; pointing across the meadows Kate said, "You can see the temple itself down there, quite marvelously preserved but never completed. The theater's up here, though, and the ruins of the town, and this I love best."

They paused at the Greek ruins of the theater, open to the sky, its rough-hewn stones set in tiers facing an empty stage, its backdrop the meadows and valleys below.

"Uncovered by archaeologists," said Kate. "You'd never know it was buried for centuries, would you? Now it looks as if at any moment people could arrive to watch a drama: one of Aeschylus', perhaps—he died in Sicily, you know."

Strolling on to the top of the hill they reached what was once the acropolis; a single line of columns stood boldly upright with nothing behind it but the blue sky, and all around, as if felled and scattered by a giant hand, lay the huge square-cut stones that had once been its walls.

"How wild and lonely," breathed Mrs. Pollifax. "And there was once a town?"

"Around here," Kate told her, and guided them over and between the great blocks of stone.

"Streets!" exclaimed Farrell, looking down a wide and grassy expanse lined with wildflowers and the ruins of walls. "Those really were streets, can you imagine what it was once like?"

"Yes," said Mrs. Pollifax contentedly. "People walked and lived and gossiped here, one can feel this. How long ago, Kate?"

"B.C. 409, roughly, at least that's when the archaeologists believe the theater was built."

Mrs. Pollifax looked out across peaceful meadows at the great sweep of checkered fields below, the curving roads white in the sunlight and the distant mountains hazy on the horizon. She drew a deep breath and said, "Thank you, Kate . . . a perfect prescription for startled nerves. I've quite recovered from what happened at the cathedral, and I think your island lovely." She added quietly, "And I think we'd better go now."

They made their way back to the car along a narrow path cut through the wildflowers, and returned to a less civilized world to hunt for Raphael's house, where Farrell had been shot.

10

Farrell had promised them a hill, and there was a hill: it slanted steeply upward to a point that overlooked the grounds on which Raphael's villa stood, and here it ended in a thirty-foot perpendicular drop down into his driveway. Two bushes had survived the hill's erosion and clung to the edge of this small precipice; from behind these, Farrell said, they could take turns observing what took place below.

"If anything takes place," said Kate wearily, dropping her knapsack to the earth.

It was already near dusk; they had pursued a network of wrong turns before finding the hill that Farrell remembered from his night visit, and then it had taken an even longer time to discover a way to reach it from the rear, after which they had left the car and walked nearly a mile, much of it uphill. The sun that had flushed Mrs. Pollifax's cheeks on their long hike was sinking now toward the grove of lemon trees beyond Raphael's villa; there was a fragrance of herbs in the air and a hint of chill. Farrell had at once positioned himself behind the denser shrub with binoculars, but Mrs. Pollifax was delighted to sit well below him and relax; it had been a strenuous afternoon, after all, and she had already examined what lay below and was satisfied. She had learned that if their view was limited they definitely had privacy; from the hill they looked down on the roof and one side of the house that held a door and three vine-covered windows. The driveway below them swept around to the front of the house, where a pair of sculptured stone lions could be glimpsed, presumably marking the front entrance. As for leaving the hill to approach Raphael's villa, once it was dark, her glance had moved to the right to find that the hill circled the rear of the grounds, gradually losing altitude until it was no more than a good jump down to a flower garden behind the house. She was content to wait.

"Have an orange," Kate said, producing several from her knapsack. "It's another hour until dark."

"Thank you," she said, and to Farrell, "Considering the events of this afternoon, isn't it time to contact Carstairs now and tell him Aristotle's here? After all, both of us have seen and identified him; what more can anyone ask?"

Farrell sighed. "Damn it, there wasn't even time to phone Ambrose Vica and tell him I'll return tomorrow, we've been so busy mingling, being shot at and finding this hill."

"Yes, but Carstairs—"

He said crossly, "I have to remind you that I'm here to search Raphael's study tonight for the Caesar document that will allow me to move *back* with Vica, who's our one link to Aristotle. It's not enough to have seen Aristotle, the guy has to be found, right? Before he shoots more people, not to mention you and me."

"Yes," said Mrs. Pollifax, "but Carstairs—"

"Have an orange," Kate told him.

Farrell absently accepted the proffered orange and dropped it to the ground. "What's more," he persisted, "once I'm back with Vica it isn't going to be easy to learn where Aristotle can be found, it's going to need *time,* and it's going to need that bloody signature of Caesar's, too."

"I don't know why you sound so cross about it," said Mrs. Pollifax. "All I suggested was that Carstairs—"

"I'm cross," he said angrily, "because I've had to sacrifice one day by spending it in hiding with an infected ankle, and I'm cross because Aristotle's seen and recognized *you,* as well as me, and *your* life's up for grabs, and maybe Kate's, too, and I don't like feeling helpless. It wasn't supposed to work out like this, it wasn't in my scenario."

"It never is," she told him, "but you can't have it both ways. When we first met two days ago you wondered if you were chasing a phantom; now I've seen him here, too, and that doesn't please you either."

Kate said brightly, "He's quite irrational, isn't he? For myself I think this is all extremely promising. You realize this assassin of yours was brought out of hiding just to follow and kill Farrell? Why else would they ever allow him out in public? I think *someone* is getting worried and wants to get the job done so they can get on with other matters. Except, of course," she added blithely, "no one figured on there being two of you now."

"You call that promising?" growled Farrell. "They'll try again, and they know exactly where to find us now. At the Villa Franca."

"Oh, Peppino won't let anyone in," said Kate serenely. "And they knew where we were, anyway."

He regarded her with suspicion. "Sally Sunshine, aren't you! *I* think the Duchess should catch the next plane out of Palermo."

"Sssh," hissed Mrs. Pollifax, "I hear a car."

Farrell returned to his binoculars while she and Kate wriggled their way up to the second bush at the edge and peered through its screen of leaves. "Mercedes," murmured Kate. "Real class."

Unfortunately the Mercedes did not stop until it had passed the two stone lions at the front of the house, and when it halted only the rear of the car was in view: it proved impossible to see whether it discharged a passenger or achieved one. After ten or fifteen minutes they heard it make its exit by an unseen road at the far side of the property. Shortly after this a man in workman's overalls emerged from a small cottage behind the house and collected a hose that had lain coiled in the garden. He too disappeared.

Mrs. Pollifax, tired of kneeling, retreated further down the hill to lie on a sparse patch of grass. The sunset's afterglow was fading, it was growing dark and already she could see a few stars glittering in the sky. A faint breeze had sprung up, threatening a cold evening ahead. She wondered what Cyrus was doing at this minute, and after computing time-changes realized that he would be sleeping; she was glad, because otherwise he would be worrying about her. The lack of a telephone at Villa Franca was annoying, but Kate had mentioned a fax machine at the local post office. Tomorrow she really must send him a message and reassure him, she thought, except how to describe what a different world she'd entered? Actually two worlds, she reflected: that of the Villa Franca—mysterious perhaps, but fortified and safe—and the world of violence and threat they faced once they left its gates.

Lest she fall asleep she sat up, and at that moment heard Kate say clearly, "We're not going to quarrel again, are we?"

Farrell's voice was low, but the quickening breeze captured his reply and sent it downwind to her. She heard him say, "You know very well that we've not been quarreling, not really."

"No?" said Kate. "What then?"

"Sounding each other out. Taking soundings like two boats in deep water."

"I avoid deep water," Kate said quickly.

"I avoid it, too. *Have* avoided, *did* avoid. Until Erice."

"Farrell, you're crazy."

"Really? Move over here to *my* bush and I'll show you how crazy I am."

"Farrell—"

"Scared?" His voice was sober.

"Of course I'm scared, I'm absolutely determined not to care about you."

"Not half as determined as I've been to not care about you. A pony-tailed CIA agent with freckles is the last thing in my scenario."

"Scenario?" Kate sounded mocking. "Well, as Mrs. Pollifax pointed out, your scenario this afternoon was—Farrell, you mustn't—*don't,* you're supposed to be watching—"

"Yes, but whenever I've been afraid of anything I find the only way to conquer the fear is to meet it. Don't you dare move, I'm going to kiss you."

"Farrell—"

A very long silence followed and Mrs. Pollifax, with a wicked smile and great tact, lay down to feign sleep for a few minutes. So *this* was what had been happening ever since Kate and Farrell met! *Miss Whatshername indeed,* she thought with amusement.

Presently when she returned to her post at the top of the hill, Kate and Farrell had primly retired to their separate bushes and were giving every attention to the scene below.

By ten o'clock three more cars had come and gone, their passengers unknown, and the house below was dark except for one light in an upstairs room, and another that illuminated the stone lions in the front. "It's time we go down," Farrell said, and drew from his pocket a gun and began loading it.

It shone brightly in the darkness, puzzling Mrs. Pollifax. "I've not seen one like that before."

Farrell grinned. "Courtesy of Kate's aunt, it's a Smith & Wesson .38 Special. Stainless steel. Neat, isn't it?" He inserted two final bullets into its cylinder. "Kate has a gun for you, too, but not loaded. I count on you for some well-placed karate strikes if necessary, but you can wave the gun around if there's trouble."

"Can we be sure there's no one at home?"

"That's what we go down to find out," he said, tucking the gun into his belt. "There could be lights on the other side." Pointing, he added, "That room on this corner is

Raphael's study where I tackle the safe again. We'll head there as soon as we've reconnoitered.''

Kate asked, ''How long do you expect it will take to learn the safe's combination and open it?''

''There's no combination, it's a very old safe that probably came with the house. Raphael had two special new locks welded into it—which he's no doubt had changed by now; I'd guess twenty minutes at the most, if they're new locks. While I'm working on it, Duchess, you stand guard at the door to the next room, which is the library. And, Kate, you make a search of the desk in the library.''

''How do we get in?'' asked Mrs. Pollifax, warming to this new role as burglar.

''The study window this time; I'll tape it with good old-fashioned flypaper, cut the glass, and the flypaper will keep the glass from falling out of its frame and noisily embarrassing us. Kate, you know what we're looking for? It needn't be more than memo-sized, definitely on papyrus, possibly with a Roman seal, and any message—if there should be one—in Greek. It would be well wrapped, probably mounted."

"Got it," nodded Kate. "Let's go."

They crept along the rim of the hill and descended to the lawn at the rear. Farrell, pointing to a hedge, whispered, "Wait," and moved toward the house; once in its shadow he could dimly be seen checking the rooms on the farther end. When he returned he said, "No lights, only the one on the second floor over the study that we saw, and of course the light at the entrance. All set? Off we go."

Leading them back to the side of the house they'd watched from the hill, they tiptoed up to the window of Raphael's study, at which point Mrs. Pollifax saw both Farrell and Kate draw out their guns and she thought with a smile, *What a suitable couple they make, working together,* and a team they definitely proved to be as Kate drew out a tiny flashlight and efficiently trained its sliverlike beam on the window. With equal efficiency Farrell taped and neatly cut out a pane of glass. Reaching inside he unlocked the window, climbed inside and helped them both over the sill.

Here they stood in darkness until Kate switched on her light, illuminating the meager furnishings of the room they'd entered: there was the safe in a corner, two armchairs, a small television set and an elaborate stereo, no more. When Kate's light found the door to the next room she grasped Mrs. Pollifax's arm and led her to her assigned post, and handing her a gun she herself disappeared into the library.

Now there was only silence and darkness until a narrow beam of light flashed across the safe and she heard Farrell say in a low voice, "Damn."

"What is it?" she whispered.

"Three locks now, all new," he whispered back, and for a moment his light remained propped on his lap while he brought out a small kit of tools. Following this the light was extinguished.

Just once she heard a rustle of movement as he moved from a crouch to a kneeling position but other than this the silence was so pronounced that when the drone of a refrigerator resumed its cycle in a distant room it caused her to jump. A glance behind her into the library showed her Kate's beam of light dancing across walls and then focusing on a desk as one drawer after another was inspected. Five minutes passed . . . ten minutes . . . fifteen . . . Kate's light was once again roaming around the walls of the library— *quite like Tinker Bell,* thought Mrs. Pollifax, repressing a sudden urge to laugh. The beam of light fell to the floor and moved nearer. "Nothing there at all," whispered Kate, touching her arm, and aimed her light at Farrell beside the safe, his fingers occupied in delicately inserting a tool into a lock, his ear pressed to the safe.

Kate's hand on her arm tightened as the safe door swung open with a creaking noise. He was about to reach inside when Mrs. Pollifax heard the distinct sound of movement in the library behind them. "Someone's coming," she whispered to Kate.

Someone was indeed coming, for a larger flashlight was sweeping the walls of the library behind them. "Tell him—he doesn't know," she whispered urgently to Kate. "I'll stay at the door and keep you covered." No sooner had Kate left her than an overhead light was snapped on in the library, bathing that room in brightness.

"Is someone there?" a woman called out sharply. "Is someone there?"

Mrs. Pollifax, still in shadow and guarding the study doorway, suddenly found the woman almost at her elbow, and looking into her face she was astonished to find it familiar.

She heard Farrell shout, "Let's *GO!*" and as the woman in the doorway fumbled for a light switch on the wall of the study, Mrs. Pollifax ran. She was the last to reach the window; the study lights were turned on just as Farrell helped her over the sill.

"Don't go!" she told him urgently, and pointed into the lighted room. "Take a good look and see who it is."

He glanced back impatiently and his jaw dropped. He gasped, "But that's Mrs. Davidson—that's *Aristotle's wife!* This is where he's been hiding, not with Vica but with *Raphael?*"

11

In Langley, Virginia, it was still early afternoon. The coup in Africa had been achieved without inordinate bloodshed, the autocratic and ailing President had fled the country, the capital was calm and Bartlett had survived the coup only a little the worse for wear from spending a night shivering in a baobab tree on the outskirts of the city. The name of the country would undoubtedly be changed again, causing grief for the mapmakers, but Bartlett was safe, the President had not been a very good president and the young rebel leader showed signs of being an improvement, at least for the moment.

This left Bernard of the Sûreté to deal with, and Carstairs was now fielding still another indignant phone call from Paris. "I'm telling you again, Bernard, that three of my agents are involved in this," he reminded him, "and you've got to give me time to hear from them and pull them off the job. I can tell you *only* that Aristotle's been sighted on an island off Italy: if I name the island you'll have your men swarming all over it, my three agents could be killed and Aristotle could get spooked and vanish again."

He glanced at Bishop seated across the desk from him and shrugged expressively. "Yes, Bernard," he said, resuming his end of the conversation, "Yes I do realize it's *your* prison he left, and *your* country that's responsible for this—er—monumental error —but it's *my* agents who spotted him—or feel sure they have—and there's been no confirmation yet, and it's placed them in a very tricky and dangerous situation . . . Where are they? At the moment I frankly don't know, which is why—" He stopped to listen impatiently, and then, "What I suggest, Bernard, is that you station your men in Italy, ready to make a move once the situation's been clarified. I need twenty-four hours, Bernard, I insist on twenty-four hours for the sake of my people . . . Yes, I know how many islands there are . . . Place your men near an airport, have a plane ready, put them on alert, and give me my twenty-four hours."

He hung up with a sigh. "He's agreed. Reluctantly."

"You're banking on the three of them being still alive, then."

"Until proven otherwise, yes, and we have to give them time. Obviously they've stirred up a hornet's nest, which has to mean they've been on Aristotle's trail."

"And he on theirs?"

"Yes," Carstairs said, and seeing the red light blinking ferociously on his phone he picked up the receiver. "Carstairs here."

At once his face changed; to Bishop he said quickly, "It's Henry Guise," and Bishop reached over and turned on the recording machine and picked up a set of headphones.

Henry Guise sounded even more aggrieved today than on his previous call; he was saying, "This Pollifax looked such a gentle, harmless little lady, you didn't tell me she was violent."

Bishop cut in eagerly to say, "You've found her? She's safe? She's all right?"

"That," said Carstairs coldly, "was my assistant speaking. Are you telling me, Guise, that you found Mrs. Pollifax?"

"Found her!" he said indignantly. "She hit me over the head and knocked me out. If Mr. Vica hadn't walked his guest to the front gate and found me I'd have frozen to death by morning. What kind of person *is* this dame, anyway?"

"Accomplished," said Carstairs dryly. "Where did this happen?"

"You told me to check out Mr. Vica's house—and a real palace it is, too, I can tell you. So I hung around there for hours, keeping my eye out for her and the Rossiter girl and for the man they collected in Erice. I was about to give up—nearly midnight, you see—when darned if I didn't see two people casing the place. The man climbed a balcony and went inside, the woman looked in windows, and I could see it was Pollifax."

Bishop chuckled, but given a reproachful

glance from his superior he made no comment.

"Go on," said Carstairs.

"As instructed, I kept my eye on Mrs. Pollifax, and when she headed for the driveway I followed. I lost sight of her down near the gates, I walked past a hedge and—pow, I got clobbered."

"By Mrs. Pollifax?"

"By her, yes. Just a glimpse, see, but it was her shape, and then I was out like a light. When I came to I was in a bed and it was daylight. It seems this Mr. Vica heard me groan when he walked past—and a good thing I did!—and it was one of his beds I woke up in, but where Pollifax and her friend went I don't know."

"Nevertheless, we're very glad to hear that she's alive and operative," Carstairs said crisply, "and it's urgent that you find her again because we've fresh information that she and Rossiter and their companion *must* be told. This is vital. She's obviously not at Vica's home. I want you to next try a place near Cefalù called the Villa Franca."

"Oh God," said Guise with feeling, "will she knock me out again if I find her?"

"It's karate, Guise, karate, she's taken lessons for years."

"Brown belt," put in Bishop happily.

"Oh God," he said again.

"Cheer up," Carstairs told him, "this time you can identify yourself—"

"If she'll give me the chance," he said gloomily.

"—because it's become a life-and-death matter now, and she absolutely must be warned—her companions, too—or next time she may *not* be found. Hold on a minute . . . Bishop, the address Rossiter left for contact?" Bishop handed him the slip of paper. "Here we are—there's no telephone so you'll have to get directions from the post office in Cefalù, roughly forty miles east of Palermo. No address, just Villa Franca, it's where Rossiter was staying on holiday, and it's how we contacted her earlier, through the post office."

Guise sighed heavily. "All right: post office, Cefalù, Villa Franca. And if I find her there's a message?"

"Yes, ready? . . . Good . . . Message as follows: ARISTOTLE NO LONGER IN FRANCE, RELEASED FROM PRISON, UR-

GENT YOU CONTACT ME AT ONCE." With a twist that he hoped she and Farrell would appreciate he said, "Add to that SOS MAYDAY MAYDAY. Got that?"

Guise read it back to him and it was pronounced accurate. "But she had no right to knock me out," he said reproachfully.

"No, but she didn't know who you were," Carstairs reminded him. "Let's hope you find her before she gets into any more trouble."

The connection severed, Carstairs shook his head. "Poor Guise, I suppose we should have warned him, but who would have thought it would have led to this?"

Bishop grinned. "Emily must be reaching black belt status by now, wouldn't you say?"

"No doubt, but I'd like to know what she was doing at midnight peering into windows at Vica's estate, and who the man was who climbed onto the balcony."

"Farrell?" suggested Bishop.

"Doubtful, highly doubtful. After all, Farrell's working for Vica, he'd be living there, not climbing balconies and burglarizing the place." His phone rang again and he picked

up the receiver. "Yes?" and then, "Oh
damn." To Bishop he said, "It's Cyrus—Cyrus Reed."

"Oh-oh," Bishop said. "What are you going to tell him?"

"As little as possible. That his wife is—
well, where? One has to remember that he
insisted she not go alone."

"She scarcely appears to be alone,"
pointed out Bishop.

Carstairs sighed and nodded. "All right,
connect me, Jennie, I'll talk with him now."

A moment later he was speaking in his
smoothest voice to a concerned Cyrus, as-
suring him that Mrs. Pollifax and the agent
she was traveling with had met Farrell
safely, that all was well, and that he and
Bishop expected word at any moment that
Mrs. Pollifax would be returning to the
United States.

"I don't like your voice," growled Cyrus.
"You've heard from her? From Farrell?"

"Not personally," Carstairs told him, "but
—uh—from others who are involved."

"Still don't like your voice," Cyrus said.
"Tactful. Silky. Hiding something."

"Be patient," Carstairs told him. "No firm

news yet, Cyrus. Be patient." He rang off and made a face at Bishop. "He's too clever."

Bishop grinned. "Well, he's accompanied Emily often enough on these jaunts to know what trouble she gets into. At least she's been *sighted.* You couldn't tell him about Aristotle or he'd be on the next plane to Sicily."

Carstairs sighed. "Very tricky, Bishop, let's keep our fingers crossed and hope Guise finds her before Aristotle does. Now where are those reports on the new government in Thailand? We need some plain dull facts for the next hour or two . . ."

12

Thursday

The next morning Mrs. Pollifax sought solace by carrying her history of Sicily to the garden where she knew she would find the fragrances and the sun healing. She had not slept well, and at six o'clock had exchanged her bed for the floor, where she had practiced her yoga. After this she had heard Igeia mumbling to herself in the kitchen, and had accepted bread and cheese for breakfast, insisting that she needed nothing more. Farrell, she thought, had been considerably shaken at discovering Aristotle's wife in the wrong house, and her sudden appearance had deprived him of removing anything new from the safe as well. On the long drive back to the Villa Franca he'd said only that he had to do a great deal of thinking and sort things out; he'd repeated this dazedly a number of times.

There did seem a number of things to sort out, decided Mrs. Pollifax, as she sat in the garden near the tarragon. She herself had only temporarily put aside her unspoken uneasiness about the Villa Franca but she thought that this needed sorting out, too; Farrell in his turn must be reassessing all of his previous scenarios—to use his word—and figuring out what to do next to put Aristotle out of action before a new assassination occurred. Obviously Farrell had backed the wrong horse, which was always upsetting. He'd met with unusual stresses, too: a witch, an infected ankle, implications that he was losing his mind over a disappearing pre-Hellenic vase, and of course through all this he'd been falling in love, which was strenuous, too. Now he was going to have to transfer his modus operandi from Ambrose Vica to Raphael—Raphael, with his taut poker face and the Caesar document hidden somewhere in his house, and apparently Aristotle and his wife hidden there too.

A pair of wealthy and dangerous men, she thought; one had given Aristotle lunch, and the other had given him shelter.

And my attention has to shift now, too, she reflected, *if I'm to help Farrell as promised, and certainly of the two of us I know the better how dangerous Aristotle is, he would have killed me in Zambia if Cyrus— dear Cyrus—hadn't hurled himself at the man and thrown him to the ground.*

She sighed and opened her book to read, "Sicily, without loss of time, became the grand base for Roman attacks upon Carthaginian power in the Mediterranean. From it, in B.C. 205, Scipio set forth to subdue Carthage and Hannibal . . ."

But this isn't B.C. 205, she reflected; *Sicily is no longer a "grand base" but a neglected appendage of Italy, left to drowse in the sun with its great ruins, its violent history and its poverty, and if Franca is helping one small village into prosperity there must be dozens upon dozens—hundreds, no doubt—in despair.*

From the kitchen she heard voices; Farrell

was greeting Igeia but she did not feel like joining him yet. At the moment she was more interested in the old man who had made his way up the hill from the village, carrying a stool and a basket. He vanished behind an olive tree and then reappeared, placing his stool on the ground and testing its stability before he sat down upon it, his basket beside him. She watched him draw out a slip of paper and roll a few fingers' full of tobacco in it, screw the ends and take a few puffs. He smiled and carefully stubbed out the cigarette, tucking it into a pocket of his shabby vest. Only then did he reach into his basket and—but what, she wondered, was he planning to do in the shade of the tree, bathed in a peacefulness that was lacking, perhaps, in the village?

He did not see her. She watched, fascinated, as he methodically unpacked his basket and when its contents surrounded him—jars of several sizes, brushes and knives—he slid from the stool to the earth and proceeded to move all these objects to the stool. There he sat, cross-legged on the ground. Selecting a brush and a jar from his cache he began to work, bent over what she thought from this distance might be a wood carving.

"Now that I'd like to see," she murmured, and left her chair to stroll through the garden and across the drive to approach the man.

"Signor," she said politely, and he glanced up, his face a network of fine lines in a dark face. He smiled broadly, exposing a deficiency of teeth but his smile was warm and welcoming. Vigorously nodding his head at her appearance he greeted her with a spate of incomprehensible words; she nodded back with enthusiasm, and feeling that communication had been established she turned her gaze to what work he was doing in the shade of the tree, and promptly froze in astonishment.

In his lap he held a wonderful old pottery jug with a pair of handles, one of which was loose and which he was about to repair with a touch of glue. The background of the jug was black but it radiated with exquisite amber-colored figures that circled it: Greek dancers etched in flowing robes, men reclining on couches with beards and wreaths on their heads . . . she drew in her breath sharply at the sight of this, knowing suddenly what Farrell had meant when he claimed to have seen a museum piece of Greek pottery: she was gazing on one at this moment.

She turned; Farrell had wandered out into the garden and was sniffing the air, a cup of coffee in one hand. "Farrell?" she called. When he didn't hear her she walked out into the driveway and called to him again. "There's something here you ought to see," she told him grimly, and led him back to the old man under the tree.

"What is it?" he asked. "I've no—" He stopped, staring down at the man in astonishment. He said in a strangled voice, "But that's—"

"Yes," she said.

He knelt and touched what the man held; he ran a finger reverently over its surface, a look of incredulity on his face. "Pre-Hellenic," he said simply. "Very, *very* old. Not the one I saw, but another."

Mrs. Pollifax nodded. "There's something else I'd like you to see, Farrell. In the house."

"But I was blatantly and flagrantly lied

to," he protested. "She implied I was hallucinating!"

"So you told me," said Mrs. Pollifax, "and I've been lied to, also. It's absolutely none of our business but I long to know why, and perhaps you can help *explain* why. You picked a lock last night, I want you to pick one now. *Grazie,*" she told the old man and led Farrell away.

Once out in the sunshine he said worriedly, "You pointed out that it's none of our business, Duchess, and you're right, it isn't."

"I realize that," said Mrs. Pollifax, "but I don't like mysteries, and Franca's telling such untruths is completely out of character, and I don't like that either."

He said, "It could be like opening Pandora's Box."

She nodded. "Possibly, and yet—" She hesitated. "Once back in the States I will always wonder what's been going on here, and what they're concealing. You will, too, I think, because of Kate."

He came to a full stop and stared at her. "How did you know? I thought I hid my feelings about Kate very skillfully, I certainly worked hard enough at it."

She laughed. "Oh you did, dear Farrell, but I couldn't help but overhear some of your conversation last night when we were on the hill overlooking Raphael's house."

"And Franca is Kate's aunt," he pointed out.

"Very true, but let me tell you now—there wasn't time before—that two nights ago I woke up, hearing the sound of a truck outside. Going to my window I watched three men return to the village, but not Peppino, who headed for Franca's studio, a rifle under his arm, and proceeded to knock on her door, speak to her, and then leave. This was at three o'clock in the morning. When I broached this subject the next day, mentioning a truck and voices waking me, both Franca and Peppino looked mystified and quite dramatically emphasized that there had been no truck and no people during the night."

Seeing Farrell look startled, and then thoughtful, she added, "And yesterday I glanced into Franca's studio while you and

Kate were playing poker, the door was ajar, and I don't think it's a studio at all."

Farrell frowned. "All right, you win. What is it you want me to see?"

"Her studio."

"I'm not even awake yet," he grumbled as they passed through the kitchen, empty now. "Where's Franca?"

"I don't know. Asleep, one hopes, but since it's past seven o'clock now it's probably not for long." She led him down the long flagstoned hallway, past his door and hers, and pointed to the door of Franca's studio.

"You mean I've got to hurry?"

"Definitely, yes."

With a sigh he drew from his pocket the chain that held a Swiss knife but to which various other implements had been added. "For heaven's sake keep a watch on the kitchen end of the hall, will you?" He knelt by the door and began probing the lock while she stood guard over him. After what felt an interminable length of time he rose to his feet, turned the knob and the door opened. "If Franca wants to keep secrets," he murmured, "she ought to invest in a better— What the devil!"

"Exactly," said Mrs. Pollifax.

He stood looking around him in astonishment. "This is—but what?"

"To me it looked like a laboratory."

"Not quite," he murmured. Walking over to the row of gleaming counters he peered at the glass jars lined up on the shelves, removed one and opened it. Sniffing it he nodded, opened another and sniffed this, too. "She grinds her own paints," he said, and turned to eye the huge wooden easel covered with a sheet. Moving quickly to it he said, "This ought to explain what's happening here." He reached up and drew away the cloth, dropping it on the floor.

Mrs. Pollifax gasped. Propped on the easel stood a canvas that glowed with brilliant clear colors: a café table, flowers, a man seated at the table, a background of busy wallpaper. "Matisse?" faltered Mrs. Pollifax, and then realized that it couldn't be a Matisse because the painting wasn't finished. The foreground was blank white canvas, the man at the table was only sketched in outline and lacked flesh tones, and—"For a moment I thought it was a Matisse," she said.

Farrell was studying it thoughtfully. "I think it's *going* to be a Matisse," he said dryly. "It's just not finished yet."

"No."

Scowling, he turned and strode over to the machine in the center of the room, flicked a switch, and on the large white screen that had puzzled Mrs. Pollifax on her earlier glimpse into the room there appeared a magnified, blown-up detail of the café table and wallpaper.

Farrell nodded. "She *copies* paintings! That has to be a detail of a Matisse painting on the screen, and she's copying it." He looked back to the easel and frowned. "And I have to admit it's a damn fine job. Those brush strokes are Matisse, those colors are Matisse, the technique is Matisse . . ."

"People *do* this sort of thing?"

He said scornfully, "Oh yes. Nouveau riche snobs who can't afford to bid millions for an original will pay a great deal for a really fine copy, rejecting reproductions as middle class and gauche, and heaven forbid they risk the work of a new artist!" A look of blinding revelation swept his face. "My God, Duchess—those pre-Hellenic vases! They're obviously copies, too. What Franca is running here is a—a virtual *factory* for turning out copies of whatever people will buy and she can sell."

Startled, Mrs. Pollifax said, "But is that legal?"

"It's legal so long as people know it's a copy they're buying." He stared at the painting, frowning and puzzled. "Or else," he began softly, "or else—"

"But the paint's dry," said Mrs. Pollifax, touching the canvas with one finger. "Perhaps it isn't hers. Certainly she's not been working on it lately."

Farrell said grimly, "No, she probably put it aside to finish the Correggio."

"The Correggio!" gasped Mrs. Pollifax. "You can't mean the Correggio was hers! Farrell, you're making me very nervous, I don't like this, do let's get out of here, I'm sorry I ever—"

Behind them Franca said calmly, "So you saw the Correggio, too?"

They turned to see that Franca had quietly entered the room behind them, bare-footed as usual, wearing a bright red robe, no wig this morning as yet, but blond hair streaked with gray flowing to her shoulders.

Mrs. Pollifax said quickly, "It would be ridiculous to apologize, it's too late, Franca, but we just saw a man in the olive grove mending a very old pottery jug, and I *did* hear a truck the other night, and—"

She looked amused. "Yes, Peppino gave me quite a scolding for lying to you. So what are you going to do now that you know how I make my living—report me to the police?"

Farrell looked at her thoughtfully. "It would really be the police, then? They're *not* copies?"

She said with a shrug, "It began that way. Caterina tells me you're an artist yourself, with a gallery in Mexico. I've been eavesdropping long enough to know that you were about to reach the next very logical conclusion, am I not right?"

Farrell said softly, "The Correggio was magnificent."

She nodded. "It fooled you? That too is magnificent. Thank you."

Mrs. Pollifax stammered, *"You* painted it —f-f-forged it?"

"As you see, I am in your hands completely, but I must warn you," she added carefully, "that Sicilians are hot-blooded and if it becomes known in the village what you've learned, all of them—Peppino, Nito, everyone—might prefer that you never leave here."

Mrs. Pollifax, offended, said, "You didn't have to say that, Franca, we're certainly aware that we might not be alive if you'd not given us refuge. I can't speak for Farrell, of course, but for myself—"

Farrell said with a wry smile, "She's right, of course, Franca; I doubt very much if either of us would have survived if we'd gone to a Palermo hotel. I think you also know that I care too much for your niece to expose you."

Franca sniffed. "Care? Always Americans avoid the word love!"

"They *are* forgeries?" asked Mrs. Pollifax. "Deliberate forgeries?"

She smiled faintly. "My grandfather left no money, it's true, only books, but—this will interest you, Farrell. Among them—but let me show you.''

She led them to the shelf of books, and from them drew a very old, tattered sheaf of pages bound together with hemp. ''The text is in Greek, as you can see,'' she said tenderly. ''I was curious, I was forced to learn rudimentary Greek to translate and read it. It's hundreds of years old and yet, old as it is, the monk who put down these words here writes that he copied from an even older manuscript. From it I learned how painters in medieval times sized their canvasses, mixed their egg-tempera and oil glazes. The rules and the formulas are all here, and when I found this,'' she said, turning suddenly fierce, ''I knew how I was going to save both myself and the village.''

''But this is astounding,'' Farrell said, touching a page reverently. ''What a discovery!''

''Yes.''

He added curiously, ''And you have copied *many* great paintings? Or should I say copied the techniques to make new ones?''

Ignoring his question she said, ''Probably neither of you would remember the Toasty-

Cozy ad campaign of 1974 that featured the *Mona Lisa . . .* that was *my Mona Lisa,* a perfect copy, which is when I realized the talent I had in this area."

"You began with copies," Farrell said doggedly. "And then?"

She smiled. "Then I came here to Sicily, and continued doing quite well with them— little sketches by Picasso, Modigliani, Dufy, Derain—but not well enough for my purposes, you see. And here was this marvelous centuries-old book with all its secrets, and a cooperative dealer in Palermo with connections in Rome and New York, and the village needed so much *more* money."

"So you—er—graduated?" suggested Farrell.

She nodded cheerfully. "The Correggio is my finest work," she confided, "but it was really exhausting. Very intricate, consuming work! So I decided yesterday to resume work on this Matisse and have a little rest." She added modestly, "I always place a very tiny dot in one corner of each painting so that I'll recognize them in museums."

"Museums," echoed Farrell, looking staggered, and then, as if struck by lightning he exclaimed, "That Dutch painting four years ago—a Frans Hals, wasn't it? An early Frans Hals, considered a precursor of his *Women Regents of the Old Man's Home.* The experts are still arguing over it, aren't they, some calling it fake, others insisting it's genuine? Dare I ask—" He stopped and said weakly, "But how tactless of me."

"Yes, very," agreed Mrs. Pollifax with a smile.

He rallied with dignity. "I hope you've noticed that I've not mentioned the pre-Hellenic pottery, although how you ever managed that, too, I can't imagine. I found it exquisite, and—"

He was interrupted by the clanging, heart-stopping sound of a bell outside, so loud that it reverberated through the house and rattled the glass jars on the shelf in the studio. Mrs. Pollifax jumped at the shock of it; Franca cried, "It's the emergency bell—*trouble!*" Unlocking the door to the garden she raced out of the room, her robe floating behind her.

Farrell and Mrs. Pollifax looked at each other and then rushed out to follow. Igeia had emerged from the kitchen end of the house, a dripping wooden spoon still in her hand; Kate pushed past her, still in pajamas with a rifle under her arm, and Mrs. Pollifax, seeing that neither Kate nor Franca headed for the main gate but down the hill, remembered the huge bell she'd seen attached to the raw new building. It was certainly ringing now, and as they reached the top of the hill she saw a very small and barefooted boy clinging to the rope and riding back and forth on it. A dozen women in black were circling a wagon of hay, shouting angrily and raising fists at something or someone; Peppino and another man were running in from the fields and Franca in her scarlet robe had just reached the angry women in black. As Mrs. Pollifax, Kate and Farrell joined the crowd the boy dropped the rope and the ringing ceased, replaced by excited voices shouting at Peppino and Franca, and all of them talking at once.

"What's happened?" demanded Farrell.

Franca, listening, turned and shouted back to them, "The boy Giovanni says he and his father drove through the back gate with a load of hay—" She stopped to hear more, and shouted, "This man was hiding in the hay. The boy found him, the father ran to get Peppino, Giovanni ran to the bell, the women surrounded and caught the man."

"But who is it?" called Mrs. Pollifax, wondering who could possibly have breached the defenses of the Villa Franca.

The women drew apart, and Mrs. Pollifax was literally stunned at seeing the man they confronted.

It was Aristotle.

13

Mrs. Pollifax, recovering from her astonishment, said quickly, "Search him!"

"But who is he?" asked Franca.

"A dangerous man," Farrell told her. *"Very.* Kate, you've got him covered with your rifle?"

"You bet I have."

Franca turned aside to translate for the others what had been said in English and the women eyed Aristotle with curiosity; he, however, kept his face expressionless and his eyes fixed on the hill above them, not even glancing at Peppino, who began a thorough search of his person for weapons.

"Nothing," called Peppino. "No gun, no knife."

"This has to be a trick of some kind," protested Farrell.

"Yes, but we can't stand here all day."

Mrs. Pollifax nodded. "Kate's right. Definitely we must recover from shock and take him somewhere private. Franca, do you mind—your house?"

Franca looked amused, and it struck Mrs. Pollifax how very little seemed to startle her. "Why not?" she said with a shrug, adding dryly, "He looks catatonic to me, but if he's really dangerous Igeia knows where there is rope to tie him up. Peppino, go with them and find out what this is all about, I'll join you in a few minutes. I want to thank Giovanni, he rang the bell so beautifully—and so quickly, too!"

Kate positioned herself behind Aristotle, her rifle prodding him in the spine, and the five of them made their way slowly up the hill in single file. Marching through the garden they passed Igeia, still standing by the door; they entered the kitchen and it was now that the irony of the situation occurred to Mrs. Pollifax: after all, Farrell had gone to great lengths to find Aristotle, the three of them had been pursued and shot at, and suddenly he had been delivered to them in —of all things—a wagon of hay.

They neither offered Aristotle a chair, nor did any of them sit down; he was prodded into a corner while they faced him at a distance of some six or eight feet.

"Well?" said Mrs. Pollifax.

He said stiffly, as if each word caused him pain, "I didn't know where else to turn, I need help."

"*Help?*" echoed Farrell blankly. He looked bereft of further speech, which seemed unproductive to Mrs. Pollifax, who quite understood his reaction but felt the occasion needed something more.

She said in a kindly voice, "What do you mean '*help*'?"

"Help," he repeated.

"Why?" asked Kate, looking bewildered.

"They're after me. Men. One of them's named Raphael."

"Peppino," Mrs. Pollifax said in a low voice without removing her gaze from Aristotle, "you had better double the guard at both gates."

Peppino shouted words to Igeia outside. "She will see to it," he said. "Ah, here is Franca—good!"

Franca halted in the doorway, watching.

"What is it they want of you?" Mrs. Pollifax asked Aristotle.

He spat out his reply. "They have a list— a long one."

Mrs. Pollifax said pleasantly, "A list of people for you to kill? But you've killed so many already, and you nearly killed me too yesterday."

His glance was scornful. "You think you'd be alive now if I'd aimed to kill you?"

Mrs. Pollifax regarded him thoughtfully, but Farrell, recovering, said sharply, "He's up to something, *watch out.*"

"I *am* watching," Mrs. Pollifax told him, "but he didn't come armed and he came alone, and Aristotle—Mr. Bimms, isn't it?— *why are you here?*"

"I told you, I need help," he said indignantly. "They're after me. These—these S.O.B.'s have taken me over."

"They've 'taken you over'—you mean they want you to kill more people?"

He nodded.

She said reasonably, "But you do have quite a reputation as an assassin, is that so surprising? You've killed a shocking number of valuable people and caused many tragedies."

"Of course," he said impatiently, "it's why I was in prison."

Taken aback at this she began again. "Well, then, tell us how you got here."

"Stole their car—one of them," he said, and with a jerk of his head, "It's still out there behind the wall. Was going to climb the wall but that hay wagon came along so I hid in it and sneaked in. Under the hay." He said firmly, "They're after me, I didn't know where else to go."

"But what do you want of us?" she asked.

"I want to go *back.*"

"Back where?" demanded Farrell. "I thought you just left."

Mrs. Pollifax gave Farrell a reproachful glance. "Back where, Mr. Bimms?"

"I told you. To prison. I never asked to be taken out."

"You want to go back to *prison?*" Farrell asked dazedly.

Aristotle gave him a cold glance. "I always work alone, you know that. Make a contact, find out who's to be ciphered, the rest is up to me. No interference, no more contact—never see them again—money paid into a Swiss account when the job's done. These rich bastards are all over me with advice, telling me how and when. Questions, questions, talk talk talk."

"You'd rather be in _prison?_"

"It's what I'm telling you," he said peevishly. "Always worked everything out for myself. _Carefully._ But these fools, these S.O.B.'s—" Mrs. Pollifax thought he would have spit on the floor to show his contempt if he'd been anywhere but in a strange house.

Farrell said with equal scorn, "I suppose you'll next say you've been rehabilitated and are tired of killing people and filled with remorse?"

Aristotle gave him an icy glance. "Go to hell."

Farrell nodded. "That sounds more like you."

Mrs. Pollifax, having never before had the

opportunity to converse with a killer, was curious. "You actually prefer prison?"

He shrugged. "They leave me alone." He added savagely, "I don't like people. This bunch of bastards are trying to *control* me. They crowd me, think they own me, I want to go *back.*"

Kate said angrily, "How can we even *think* of helping a professional assassin?"

Mrs. Pollifax nodded. "It does put us in a rather strange position, doesn't it? Yet he only—apparently—asks to be taken back to France and to prison."

"No, he's asking us to save his *life,*" Farrell said indignantly. "He's told us they'll be after him, he stole their car, didn't he?"

"Which," said Mrs. Pollifax, "ought to be hidden at once."

"And," continued Farrell, "I hope you heard him imply that he'd be happy to kill again if he could do it without interference and being hassled. This is a trick, I tell you, he hopes to gain our sympathy, steal Franca's car and escape the island."

"Not," said Mrs. Pollifax, "if he can be tied up and hidden here until the authorities and Carstairs can be notified." She added pointedly, "You wanted nothing more than to find him, Farrell, you've been searching for him and here he is."

Farrell made a face. "I didn't expect *this.*"

Kate grinned. "Not in your scenario?" And to Aristotle, "What about your wife? Aren't you leaving her in the lurch—abandoning her?"

He gave her a malevolent glance. "Her! She *helped* them get me here. She'll get by, she always does. Money money money!"

"We really must hide him," said Mrs. Pollifax. "That is, if a place can be found for him here. If Franca gives us permission." Turning to her she said, "He's dangerous, how do you feel about this? Is it possible? Can you spare a bedroom?"

Kate shook her head and said sharply, "He could be found in one of the rooms here, Franca, or in any obvious place. Someone might get in—or he go out."

Peppino, seeing the look she gave her aunt, said flatly, *"No, Kate!"*

No what? wondered Mrs. Pollifax.

Kate said to Franca, "It has to be a terribly *safe* place, where he's not dangerous to us and can't be found by people searching for him. When the police come for him he can be moved, he needn't be *found* there.''

"Caterina,'' growled Peppino, ''you ask too much. Look at all these people hearing you.''

Hearing what? wondered Mrs. Pollifax, thoroughly puzzled and curious now.

There was a long silence as they all turned to Franca and waited. She in turn appeared to be thinking, her glance resting first on Aristotle, then on Kate. "Peppino,'' she said at last, ''they have already seen the studio.''

"The devil they have!''

"And each has given a pledge of silence.''

Peppino's eyes narrowed; he looked long and searchingly at Mrs. Pollifax and then at Farrell, and shrugged. ''As you say, Franca.''

Franca nodded. ''Then come.''

"Come where?'' asked Farrell.

"Never mind,'' Franca told him, ''just come.''

Once again they formed a procession as Franca led them down the hallway, Farrell at her side followed by Mrs. Pollifax, Aristotle, Kate with the rifle, and Peppino bringing up the rear. They passed the living room, several closed doors, the bathroom, Farrell's room, Mrs. Pollifax's room, the office where the Correggio had been seen, and halted at the door to Franca's studio.

Drawing a scarf out of the pocket of her robe Franca handed it to Mrs. Pollifax. "You will please blindfold this man with the Greek name."

Mrs. Pollifax approached the startled Aristotle and secured the scarf around his head, after which Franca opened the door and they grouped themselves just inside the studio; removing another key from her pocket Franca unlocked the door to the closet.

Except it was not a closet, as Mrs. Pollifax had assumed, nor was it a repository holding fake Greek vases; it concealed six steps down to a landing, where more steps turned sharply to the left. Franca paused to light a lantern that waited just inside the door—*of course, the generator isn't working,* thought Mrs. Pollifax—and then Franca led them down, holding the lantern high.

Mrs. Pollifax could hear muffled complaints from Aristotle stumbling along in the rear; ahead, at the bottom of the stairs gleamed the light of another lantern that presently illuminated a very startled Nito holding a lantern in one hand and a pistol in the other.

What is *this,* she thought in alarm.

"It's all right, Nito," Franca reassured him, "there is a man to hide. Not a good man, but even worse men look for him. We must hide him until the *polizia* come to collect him."

At the base of the staircase Farrell had stopped in astonishment, so that it was necessary for him to be prodded out of the way, and then Mrs. Pollifax stepped from the last stair and stopped in astonishment, too.

She gasped, "But—is that a *mine shaft?* You have a mine down here?" She was aware of a large generator off to her left in the basement, and a huge storage tank of fuel, as well as piles of lumber and stacks of bricks but what she was staring at was the basement wall facing the stairs. There was a large gap in that wall, its opening framed and shored up by timber. A lantern just inside it illuminated a ceiling and earthen walls supported by beams, a narrow scaffolded passageway, the silhouette of a ladder and beyond this darkness. A mine, surely.

"No," said Franca calmly, "there is a two-thousand-year-old village buried under this house; we discovered it when the first generator was brought in and the wall began collapsing."

"My God," gasped Farrell, "the pre-Hellenic vases are *real?*"

She looked at him in amusement. "Yes, Farrell, they are quite real."

"Those seven men with shovels!" gasped Mrs. Pollifax. "I saw them my first morning here—your whole village is involved?"

"Of course," said Franca, "but I think we do not speak any more of this down here." She whispered words in Nito's ear and at once he dug out a canvas from the bricks and hung it over the excavation's entrance to conceal it. She nodded. "Guard him, Nito, until we bring down rope and a chair for him. You can remove his blindfold now, too."

Aristotle said defiantly, "I need nothing. No rope, no chair."

"You will have both," Franca told him firmly. "We go."

Still somewhat stunned they were led up the stairs by Franca, through the studio and down the long hall to the kitchen, where Igeia gave them accusing glances as she poured coffee, muttering under her breath.

Ruefully Mrs. Pollifax said, "Franca, we have completely disrupted your life."

Franca only shrugged. "What happens, happens; who can complain? The gods test us."

"But it's exciting," Farrell said, thoroughly recovered now. "What a find, Franca! I hope you'll let us see the—they're called digs, aren't they? Except"—he frowned—"it's a very delicate process, excavating, isn't it? Aren't you afraid the workers will step on something, crush an artifact, be clumsy?"

Franca smiled at Peppino. "It was a very small generator, that first one, remember Peppi? All I could afford at that time. The vibrations shook the wall and it crumbled, but when we discovered what lay behind it and below us—what a moment!—we had a meeting, the whole village. It was decided that Peppino must go to Syracuse to learn about such matters, and so for a year he worked as laborer with an archaeologist, and when he came back he taught the rest of us."

"But this is amazing," said Mrs. Pollifax. "And to realize the Greeks were living *under* you two thousand years ago."

Farrell looked at Kate with interest. "You've known this?"

She nodded. "Of course."

"There hasn't been much excavating done in Cefalù," Franca added, "but it's known that it was once an ancient Sikel city named Cephaloedium. It's first mentioned in a 396 B.C. treaty by that name, and it's known that later it was captured by Dionysius of Syracuse in 307 B.C. Kate has been *such* a help researching the area, not here in Sicily, of course, but in the United States."

"Oh?" said Mrs. Pollifax. "To keep it secret, I suppose?"

Kate said with feeling, "Just to survive here Franca has to—"

"Kate!"

"Well, why not say it? There aren't just taxes but—well, certain extra payments—so no one will be too curious."

Mrs. Pollifax said matter-of-factly, "The word is bribe, I believe."

"Contributions," Franca said politely.

Mrs. Pollifax didn't ask if private excavations on the island were legal; legal appeared to be a word that was not familiar to Franca at all. Instead she said firmly, rising from her chair, "I think it's time we find that telephone and put in a call to Carstairs about Aristotle in the basement. I'd like to cable Cyrus, too."

"Oh dear, I'm still in pajamas," lamented Kate. "I'll get dressed and fetch the car, but will it be safe? Do you think they followed Aristotle here? He wasn't at all clear about that. Perhaps I should make the call and the two of you stay here."

Farrell grinned. "No one—but *no one,* my dear Rossiter—is going to deprive me of telling Carstairs what's happened. We'll take guns with us and chance it. Carstairs *has* to be notified or Aristotle will put down roots and grow mold in Franca's cellar. He's got to be removed—let's go!"

*   *   *

Cefalù was full of sun and people and the sea was blue and the sky cloudless; Mrs. Pollifax thought it an absolutely delightful seaside town to explore but for the moment she could only be grateful that they'd left the Villa Franca without being seen, although each of them knew they might not be so fortunate on their return. They parked at a hotel near the promenade and smuggled Farrell into the lobby, standing guard beside him while he made his call.

It was the middle of the night in Virginia, but in Baltimore Jennie was at the switchboard and said at once that she'd connect Farrell with Carstairs at his home. "Although he may be a bit cross, he usually is when woken up."

Carstairs was not at all cross, however. "Thank God you're alive and safe," he said with feeling, "and if you've found Aristotle as well, that's incredible. I won't ask how, there's no time, it's been difficult protecting you from the French, who have wanted to take over, or bring in Interpol; I've advised

Bernard at the Sûreté to position his men in Milan all set to move. If they're in place by now they *could* be in Sicily in a matter of hours unless they run into clearance problems. Now tell me precisely where you are, I'm going to contact Bernard immediately . . ."

Putting down the phone, Farrell was puzzled. "He was certainly fervent about learning we're alive and safe. He seemed to know a great deal of what's been going on here, but there wasn't time to ask how. It's the French—or Interpol—who will be coming."

"Not so loud," cautioned Kate.

"Well, it's a French prison he returns to," Mrs. Pollifax pointed out sensibly, and claimed her turn at the phone. Feeling that an actual conversation with Cyrus would take too much time, as well as reveal too much to alarm, perplex and distract him she reduced her message to a cable that read simply ALL WELL STOP HOPE TO JOIN YOU SOONEST STOP LOVE EMILY. There seemed no point in confiding to him that she and Farrell had met with Aristotle again, had been waylaid

by hoodlums, or that she had added burglary to her list of experiences.

They were able to return successfully to
the Villa Franca, and—lest Aristotle remain
upset—she thought he would appreciate
learning that his hours in the cellar were limited and that he would presently be restored to prison, an ambition that seemed
to her extremely odd, and about which she
admitted some skepticism despite his obvious sincerity at six o'clock that morning.

Now, however, it was just past noon, and
she was curious as to whether he had re-
considered his reckless escape from
Raphael.

*   *   *

For lunch Igeia served a spectacular minestrone soup that was accompanied by
slabs of her freshly baked herb bread with a
side dish of chick-pea fritters that Kate
called _pannelle._ "I think," said Mrs. Pollifax,
"that I would like to take Aristotle's lunch
down to him, it's possible that Igeia's food
may thaw him out enough so that he'll _talk._
Igeia is a wonderful cook."

"She's Nito's grandmother," Kate said,
"and cousin to Peppino's wife Sandrina,

and when she knows you better she may even make for you *pasta con le fave.* If you're volunteering to go down, send Nito up for his lunch, will you?"

Mrs. Pollifax agreed to this, and made her way carefully down the stairs to the basement, balancing Aristotle's lunch on a tray and relieved to see that a lantern had been left burning at the foot of the steps. Reaching it she noticed the curtain had been removed from the entrance to the excavations but there was no sign of either Nito or Aristotle.

Alarmed, she stood next to the flickering light and said, "Mr. Bimms? Nito?"

A muffled grunt came from the left corner of the basement and, much to her surprise, she saw that a new wall of bricks, roughly six feet high, had appeared there since their earlier visit. Picking up the lantern Mrs. Pollifax advanced toward the wall in search of the grunt that had apparently emanated from behind it. She found the wall solid and doorless but peering around its one exposed side she saw an opening and carried both tray and lantern to it.

And there was Aristotle seated on a chair

with a book in his lap, a small pocket flashlight trained on its pages. By the light of the lantern she was amused to see that it was the history of Sicily that she had been struggling through, but the wall startled her.

"This wall, Mr. Bimms," she began.

He glanced up, his eyes hostile. "Yes. A wall."

"Lunch," she said, and put down the tray. "It wasn't here before—the wall," she repeated.

"No."

Backing out, lantern in hand, she was just in time to see Nito emerge from the excavation with his own lantern. "This wall, Nito," she began again.

Nito shrugged. "He insisted, Signora. He sees the bricks, he begins . . . one on top of one, two on top of two. Then he go in and sit. There was no refusal, you understand? So what the hell, he sits. I gave him the pocket flashlight, he ask for a book."

"Strange," murmured Mrs. Pollifax.

Nito nodded. "Beats *me.* There being no need to sit with the gun, I do a little work. But you understand I keep the ears open—and the key to the door in my pocket."

"Very wise," she agreed, frowning.

"Like my little cousin," he said with a smile. "She makes the house out of cardboard, she make a nest. And sits."

"Yes," murmured Mrs. Pollifax. *Or like a cell,* she thought, puzzled. "Well, I was to tell you that your lunch is ready, and I'm to guard our prisoner while you're gone."

He left her wondering what such a confining space could bring to Aristotle to be so valued. It could, she supposed, be called the equivalent of a womb except that it was obviously the walls that mattered: walls that kept out the world? in which case, perhaps, they enlarged the person inside of them, so that the very smallness of space could be the ultimate security, a completely governable and controllable environment. It might be like that, she thought. Tomblike, of course, but orderly and above all safe from *people.* And Aristotle had made it clear that he did not like people.

He would have to tolerate her invading that space now, she decided, and carrying several bricks on which to sit, she placed them in the doorway and sat down. Ignoring his frigid glance she said, "The car you came in, and left at the back gate, has been moved and hidden but I'd like to ask what you expect Raphael or his men to do next. Will they have any idea that you might be here at the Villa Franca?"

He said indifferently, "Oh yes."

Startled, she said, "Why?"

He plucked a chick-pea fritter from the plate with his fork and examined it with interest. "Because I was to shoot and kill Mr. Farrell this morning and get it over with. Kaput. Because they didn't like my shooting at you instead. Because hearing that you knew me they didn't like my not killing *you.*"

"Out of practice?" she suggested dryly. "You missed me."

"Out of practice?" he repeated angrily. "Try me! Give me a gun, take me outside and I'll show you who's out of practice." The chick-pea fritter went into his mouth and he chewed it appreciatively. "Anyway, I heard them talking about this so I walked out, found a car with keys in it and took off. They heard and followed. Lost them a mile or two back but—" He shrugged. "They wouldn't *know,* but they must suspect."

There was silence while Mrs. Pollifax thought about this disconcerting news. "I would think they'd try the airports and the ferries first," she ventured.

He said calmly, "No money, no passport. *And I didn't kill you.*"

"That's a basis for friendship?"

He recoiled at the thought, giving her a look in which she read pure hatred. There would have to be a different approach, and remembering how meticulously Aristotle's plans for assassinations had always been made and carried out she decided to tap this grotesque skill. "Then tell me, Mr. Bimms," she said, "what would *you* plan next if you were Mr. Raphael?"

"Raphael!" He spat out the word with contempt but she had reached him with this appeal; his eyes were no longer stony but turned inward, he was thinking about what she'd asked and the difference in his expression was palpable. Obviously Aristotle liked *plans.* After a moment he nodded. "If it were me—but they're *not* me," he said with satisfaction. "Knowing them and their ways—bah—they'll wait for dark and use force. Force," he repeated scornfully.

"Those two gunmen—crude. No subtlety. Don't know the word preparation."

On this subject Aristotle was no longer given to monosyllables. "And that," she said conversationally, "was how you planned your—er—assassinations? With subtlety and preparation?"

His eyes lit up with pleasure. "For days, months . . . to create perfection needed research and planning, it was everything."

"The *killing* was nothing?" she said, considerably jarred.

"Only completion," he said dismissively. "The planning—now there was the challenge. Creative. Intricate. So many calculations: trajectory, distance, the proper weapon, the disguise, the getaway. Timing had to be *perfect,* you understand, worked out mathematically like a geometry problem . . . Yes, like a geometry problem . . . *Hours* of calculations and numbers. Everything computerized. I liked that."

"You didn't," she said, "feel any emotion about killing another human being?"

He looked at her blankly. "Killing? I shot them, that's all, it's what I got paid to do."

She shivered and realized that she didn't

care to hear any more, but there was one more question to ask. "Were you in solitary confinement while in prison?"

The wisp of a smile tugged at his lips. "I made sure of it."

She nodded and stood up, taking the tray from him. Curtly she said, "The authorities have been notified, you won't have long to wait."

Leaving, she was relieved to see Nito descending the stairs. "You okay?" he said in surprise, seeing her face.

"I don't know," she told him. *Murders like a geometry problem, people reduced to numbers without personality, warmth or heart . . . but of course,* she thought, *numbers—unlike people—were impersonal, reliable, predictable, stable and above all tidy.*

She felt a little sick. "I just need some fresh air," she told Nito, and went upstairs to tell the others of the most important information that she had gleaned from Aristotle: that quite possibly Raphael knew where he was and would make an attempt to recover him by force once it was dark.

14

She found franca in the kitchen slicing tomatoes. "To dry in the sun," she explained, and then, hearing of Aristotle's supposition she sighed. "Oh damn. Of course I hoped— but we'll call a meeting at once and begin plans in case he's right, and Peppino must go to the *carabinieri*—we have a friend there, an uncle of little Giovanni who rang the bell this morning. I *hate* guns," she said. "The last time a mob tried to get inside the walls Gino Trabia had to have a bullet dug out of his arm. Who is this Raphael?"

"We don't know," Mrs. Pollifax told her. "Farrell was hired by Mr. Vica, Ambrose Vica, to—uh—retrieve a historical document from Mr. Raphael, and it was in doing this that Farrell was shot. It had nothing to do with Aristotle," she added, and remembering Franca's subtle reaction earlier to the name of Ambrose Vica she said casually, "You've met Mr. Vica?"

Franca shrugged. "In the art world he is well known. Now if you'll excuse me I'll ring the emergency bell and call a meeting."

As solace Mrs. Pollifax called after her, "The law's been notified, you know, and they may arrive long before Raphael tries anything, they may even be on their way now."

"From where?" asked Franca skeptically.

"The law in Sicily, for instance, is dependable only to a certain point. There are some good police, and some not so good. You had better warn Farrell and Kate, they're in the garden."

Mrs. Pollifax glanced at her watch. Only four or five hours to darkness, she realized, and whether Aristotle was right or not about Mr. Raphael it was obvious that a sleepless night lay ahead of them. She walked out into the sunny garden and saw Farrell and Kate seated companionably in the shade,

Farrell gesturing dramatically and Kate laughing.

Seeing her, Kate said, "I'm envious, Mrs. Pollifax! He's just been describing how the two of you met, first in Mexico and then in Zambia—no wonder you're such firm friends! Do pull up a chair and join us."

"I'd love to," she told them, "but there's no time for it—Franca's on her way down the hill to ring the emergency bell."

"She's *what?*"

Mrs. Pollifax nodded. "When I confronted Aristotle in his den at lunch—and he's made himself a very *small* den—he was quite sure that Raphael will guess where he is and come for him after dark." She added carefully, "Of course he may be wrong."

Farrell said grimly, "Not if Raphael knows that he's here. What makes Aristotle think that?"

She explained in detail what he'd told her. "It's because he didn't kill either of us, you see, which I have to say was quite astonishing to me at the time; inexplicable, actually. I can understand it better now: in that calculating mind of his he was already struggling to find a way to escape Raphael.

They should have kept him hidden! Seeing me, he decided I might be useful if he didn't eliminate me."

"How coolly you say the word eliminate," Kate said with a shiver.

Mrs. Pollifax smiled. "It's an Aristotle word, isn't it, removing all emotion from the word kill. I must still be down in the cellar listening to him, but in any case it certainly aroused suspicions, my remaining alive."

Kate said soberly, "Just think of the fortune they must have invested in getting him out of prison, out of France and into Sicily— they won't just let him disappear."

"Then what—" began Farrell, only to be interrupted and silenced by the ringing of the great bell. When its noise had subsided he said, "What happens next, Kate? Should we go down and join Franca?"

"No, they'll be coming up here once they're in from the fields . . . Peppino, Vincenzo, Gino and Pasquale, and possibly Manfredi. The planning committee."

"And how many men should we expect Raphael to round up for a visit to the Villa Franca after dark?" asked Farrell quietly.

Kate considered this. "If he only leased

his villa, then his connections with the natives would be poor, although of course money can buy almost anything. There are the two apaches, one of them shot in the hand."

"Also that mysterious chap who was stalking the Duchess at Vica's. Guise was his name, wasn't it?"

Mrs. Pollifax nodded. "Henry Guise. There was also a gardener glimpsed at Raphael's."

Farrell added in a hard voice, "And possibly Ambrose Vica would contribute some men, depending on how close he and Raphael are . . . He just *could* supply more men if they're in this together."

"But in what together?" asked Mrs. Pollifax. "That remains the mystery. What assassinations have been planned, and why?" Since neither of them knew the answer she turned to Kate to ask how many people lived in the village below.

Kate grinned. "I can rattle that off for you: population two hundred and seven; twenty-three families, a lot of children, and fifty-eight adult men and women, fifteen of them quite elderly."

"And a hell of a lot of wall to defend," pointed out Farrell, looking somber. "And if it's dark?"

"There should be a bright half-moon tonight, God willing," said Kate. Rising from her chair she said, "I think I'll go down and have a little talk with Norina."

"The resident witch?" asked Mrs. Pollifax alertly.

Farrell said, "Kate, you surely don't believe—"

"We need a moon," she told him, smiling, and left them presently to vanish down the hill.

*   *   *

Five men sat at the long table in the kitchen, dominated by a patriarchal elder with a worn and craggy face and a sweeping heroic mustache. "That's Manfredi," whispered Franca from the doorway where she and Mrs. Pollifax stood to watch. "He's clever and experienced, he has fought in real wars."

Nito had been replaced in the basement; he arrived breathlessly, carrying a map that he at once unfurled and spread out on the table. The men leaned over it, each speaking with passion but in Sicilian.

"It's the map of our property," said Franca. "With small x's showing guard posts established long ago. Come and help me collect the guns from the living room."

They moved down the hall to the living room, and Franca stood on a stool to remove the guns over the mantel and hand them down to Mrs. Pollifax. "But surely these aren't the only guns available?" she asked.

"Oh no, these are only di Assaba guns, the village guns and the ammunition are locked up in the schoolroom. That's what Kate and Farrell are helping distribute down the hill."

"Yes, but what if there's no moon?" she asked. "You've no electric lights, how will you see anyone climb over a wall?"

Franca smiled. "Ah, but there are booby traps along three of the walls—what time it needed to acquire so many tin cans! Nothing here gets thrown away. They hang there —with cut glass lining the tops of the most distant walls. For the long front wall we turn on the headlights of the tractor, and of my car. Every villager has a flashlight, too, a good one, and we own six walkie-talkies. If the generator is kind to us, and there remains enough fuel, we will have one big floodlight to turn on, but only if real trouble comes. This is placed up here at the top of the hill, and lights up the village and both rear and front gates."

"I see," said Mrs. Pollifax, frowning.

"And," said Franca with a twinkle, "we also have three very old bicycles on which messengers carry communications should a walkie-talkie fail."

"Oh well then," Mrs. Pollifax said, beaming at her, "that makes *everything* all right."

Franca laughed.

"But what about the—well, the other times?" asked Mrs. Pollifax, curious.

Franca shrugged. "The first time people came over the walls we were lucky, they got in, but they were poor and hungry people and we fed them, showed them what we were trying to do here, and they left peaceably. The second time—" She sighed. "We were better prepared, there had been rumors, but it was a vicious group of men. They didn't expect us to have guns and we sent them flying, but knowing who was behind it—I mention no names—we took our complaint to the *carabinieri* and—well, certain arrangements were made that we could live in peace, at least from *them.* Those were not good days! The other times—well, we learned how to protect ourselves. It's better now, people leave us alone, they know we put our money into the farm and are not rich, but I long for a day when there'll be no need for walls and guns anywhere.''

"I think you're *very* rich," Mrs. Pollifax told her softly, and carried six of the guns out of the room before Franca could reply.

*   *   *

An hour later, in the heat of the afternoon, the tractor roared up the hill and was carefully distanced in front of the main gate. Franca's car disappeared to a position further down the wall. Mrs. Pollifax, wandering down the hill to the village, noticed several women loading guns and rifles, while little Giovanni-of-the-bell-ringing was happily ensconced on one of the ancient bicycles and riding furiously up and down the lane. Of Farrell there was no sign, but at the last house she found Nito and Kate seated on the doorstep checking the six walkie-talkies.

Kate looked up with a smile. "It's a relief to find they all work; no one has come over the walls for two years."

"Three," corrected Nito.

"How can I help, what can I do?" asked Mrs. Pollifax.

Kate grinned. "Franca has plans for you, did you doubt it? She has plans for everyone; she and Peppino know that you can shoot but don't like guns. Can you ride a bicycle?"

Startled, Mrs. Pollifax said, "Up- or downhill?"

Kate laughed. "Downhill. Franca's learned you know karate. If there really should be an attack she doesn't want anyone badly hurt, shot, or hit over the head with a gun, she'd rather they just be stunned."

"Oh," said Mrs. Pollifax, blinking.

"You're to be posted on the hill with Peppino and his walkie-talkie and one of our three bicycles. In case anyone gets in you'll be available and mobile. Farrell has been assigned the important post on the west corner of the property with four men, I'll be in the east corner over beyond the lemon grove with Maria, Nito, Gino and Blasi. There'll be others stationed at points in between but we've not enough people between the main gate and the back gate."

Mrs. Pollifax looked at little Giovanni pedaling furiously up and down the lane and considered pointing out that she'd not ridden a bicycle in years but this seemed a tactless response, especially since the possibility looked infinitely remote that she'd be needed when some forty men and women would be manning the barricades. She thought it quite likely that this was Franca's somewhat devious method of keeping her out of the way, and so she nodded and said cordially that she was delighted to be of help and would do her best. With this stated she strolled back toward the road up the hill, pausing halfway down the lane when the sound of a steadily humming voice met her ears. Peering around the side of the house she saw a young woman crouched over a tub of water, stirring the water with her fingers, stopping to drop a handful of flowers into it and murmuring incantations over it with her eyes closed.

Norina, summoning the moon, guessed Mrs. Pollifax and continued up the hill.

* * *

For dinner Igeia merely reheated the minestrone, removed her apron, picked up a gun and walked out. No one talked or ate much; it was possible that no one in the village had an appetite either; everyone waited in considerable suspense for the sun to drop below the horizon.

As it grew dark Mrs. Pollifax, watching from the hill, saw flickers of light like fireflies descend on the lane below as flashlights moved out of houses, some to disappear behind the lemon grove, others to fan out across the fields. One small group climbed the hill to guard the gate and its wall, and Mrs. Pollifax wished them a good evening as they passed. They gravely nodded, giving her and the bicycle beside her furtive, interested glances before they vanished into the darkness behind her. She did not know whether to feel amused or in awe over these simple archaic arrangements that saw an entire village leaving their homes to fight invasion. There was something medieval about it and endearing, and she could only pray that if Raphael *did* try to invade the Villa Franca no one would be hurt. She hoped that Norina's incantations had included this plea; so far they had not produced a moon. It had risen on schedule, Mrs. Pollifax had seen it, but almost at once it had been obscured by mischievous clouds.

The attack began at half-past eight, proving Aristotle's assassinlike cunning to be accurate. It began at the front gate, where the headlights of the tractor illuminated a man suddenly appearing on top of the wall. He was met with shouts, and the floodlight was at once turned on by Franca, the man retreated and the floodlight was extinguished. After this only the tractor's beams pierced the darkness but their glow didn't reach the farmhouse or the hill where Mrs. Pollifax stood beside her assigned bicycle, not far from Peppino holding his walkie-talkie. The walkie-talkie crackled and Mrs. Pollifax could hear unintelligible words. Peppino called to Franca in the doorway, "Tony reports eleven other men at the gate when the man climbed up. They have two ladders."

"Oh-oh," said Franca.

A tiresome and suspenseful silence followed, made more endurable by the moon finally appearing from behind the clouds; it shone on the village, silvering the tile roofs; a dog barked, and then a rattle of gunshots broke out, muffled by distance. In the moonlight Mrs. Pollifax saw young Giovanni pedal fast toward the lemon grove; he was gone in two blinks of an eye. This time Mrs. Pollifax recognized Kate's voice on Peppino's walkie-talkie, and he shouted to Franca, "Six men all at once along the wall in the west corner. Caterina says they hit one of the men in the arm, all six driven back."

"But only six," responded Franca. "The other six?"

"Will be heard from soon enough," said Peppino.

Mrs. Pollifax gripped the handlebars of the bicycle out of sheer nervousness. Occasionally someone turned on a flashlight down by the pond to inspect a section of wall, but very seldom because the light of the moon was sufficient now. Suddenly she heard a series of shots from the opposite direction, in the west, followed by silence, more shots and again silence. This time it was Farrell's voice on the walkie-talkie and Peppino called out to Franca, "They've tried the west side. Two men got over the wall, our people shot over their heads, the two were pulled back by their comrades. Nobody wounded. There were six, Farrell says. All clear now."

Franca left the doorway to join him, looking worried. "So far they've only searched for a weak spot—six here, six there. One can guess what next."

Peppino nodded and crossed himself.

By the light of the moon little Giovanni was seen pedaling furiously back again on his bicycle; he passed the rear gate and continued along the path to the reservoir and out of sight. *Our courier,* thought Mrs. Pollifax with a smile. Ten minutes later the bicycle could be seen returning but not with Giovanni.

"That's Farrell," called out Mrs. Pollifax in surprise.

He jumped from the bicycle at the gate

just as two dark figures hurried toward him from behind the lemon grove.

"That's Kate and Blasi," Peppino said. "Something's happening."

"I don't hear anything."

"Too far away, but there must be trouble at the gate. It's only built of wood, Franca." He handed her the walkie-talkie. "I'm going down."

"Yes," she said.

Mrs. Pollifax watched him hurry down the hill and break into a run once he reached the village; something was obviously wrong because several men stationed in the fields were also running toward the gate.

Franca's hand tightened on the walkie-talkie. "Calling Farrell, calling Kate, calling Blasi . . ."

Kate's voice answered. "We're trying to be very quiet, Franca, they were overheard planning the back gate next, all of them, and they're working on it now, one can hear them. We thought of men going over the wall to fight, but—hang on, they're still deciding."

"That gate," murmured Franca, and shook her head. "You can hear," she added, holding up the walkie-talkie for Mrs. Pollifax to listen. "They're hammering at the center. Mercifully they've not thought of a battering ram."

From the walkie-talkie came Farrell's voice loud and clear. "Send Mrs. Pollifax down, Franca—*fast!*"

Franca gave her a quizzical glance. "Well?" she said.

Mrs. Pollifax drew a deep breath. "Yes," she said, and mounting the bicycle braced herself and let go, propelled down the steep hill with the speed of a comet and hanging on for dear life as the bicycle met with pebbles, small stones and grassy mounds. Her ride carried her halfway through the village lane before her feet had to grope for the pedals again, and although the brakes were in need of repair she managed to hit no one, and arrived at the gate only a little out of breath.

"Well done, Duchess," Farrell said with a grin. "You've heard? If not, you can hear them now, hammering and sawing away at the bolts. We need you. Hell to pay if they open the gate, come inside, we shoot and they shoot. We've a better plan."

"Such as what?" asked Mrs. Pollifax with interest, leaning her bike against the wall.

"Such as enough men lined up to keep the gate from opening more than a few feet so that only one of these hoodlums can enter at a time. One at a time . . . _only one,_" he emphasized. "Blasi's calling in more men."

Mrs. Pollifax understood at once. "And there'll be enough men and muscle to keep the gate from opening wider? They mustn't come through too fast!"

"I promise—and we'll be the second line of defense just in case," he assured her. "The important thing is to prevent any shooting."

"Yes," she said, already reviewing pressure points in her mind. "Then if you'll tell me exactly where you want me placed—?"

* * *

They waited; the sound of saw and hammer was less muted, wood was splintering and the gate being wedged open. A dozen men of the village were lined up now to hold the gate; Mrs. Pollifax, positioned at the widening crack in the center, summoned energy, planted her feet firmly, and flattened her right hand for a karate chop. *"Hi-ya,"* she whispered fiercely to herself. *"Hi-YA!"*

Twelve men outside the wall pushed hard against the gate to thrust it open; twelve men inside the wall braced themselves against the pressure, and with toes dug into the earth they halted the gate's opening beyond Farrell's prescribed two feet. "Keep leaning," Farrell whispered. "Lean *hard.*"

A man in an orange shirt entered sideways through the narrow opening, arriving conveniently at Mrs. Pollifax's elbow. She was ready with a quick side-kick to his ankle and a karate chop to the side of his neck; he gasped and began a slow and silent descent earthward: Peppino neatly caught him, lifted him to one side and waited for the man who confidently and innocently followed.

Really it was quite exhilarating, thought Mrs. Pollifax, dazzled by the rapidity with which they continued to arrive and by the rapidity with which they fell. It began to have the feel of a scene from an early Chaplin film, so unknowingly did they slip through the opening to be knocked over like tenpins. She was fully prepared to dispatch the twelfth and last intruder when a shout came from Franca up on the hill.

"Peppino! Kate! Everyone! Sergeant Pirello is here—police!"

The fallen men were beginning to stir and moan. With a laugh Kate seized Farrell's walkie-talkie and called, "Wonderful! Give him all the smelling salts you have in the house, Franca, and send him down to us."

15

Friday

It was midnight, and quiet had descended upon the Villa Franca and the village below. Mrs. Pollifax, Kate and Farrell sat at the long kitchen table sipping cups of cocoa; Peppino was out making sure that a guard remained at each gate, and Franca was still down in the village where Nito had brought out a few bottles of homemade wine to toast the success of the evening. No strangers remained in the village other than Aristotle, in temporary residence in the basement; Mrs. Pollifax had taken food down to him but had found him sound asleep, which she did not think surprising because in his hand he still clutched *The*

History of Sicily, a perfect prescription, she felt, for any insomniac.

The three of them were contemplating Farrell's succinct, "Now what?"

And none of them had an answer to this.

Except to wait for Aristotle to be removed from the Villa Franca.

"Which doesn't solve who brought Aristotle to Sicily, and for what," Farrell said wearily.

"We're tired," said Mrs. Pollifax. "It's been a long day and we need sleep."

"Who could possibly sleep?" he said crossly.

Mrs. Pollifax felt that she could sleep very well indeed, and would be grateful for the opportunity, but she did not want to be unsympathetic or rude. Under the table she massaged the hand that had karate-chopped eleven men—it ached—and tried to conceal a yawn. "It went off surprisingly well," she said, "but surely this can be continued tomorrow?"

Farrell glanced at his watch and smiled. "Duchess, it already *is* tomorrow, it's 12:04."

"I'm sleepy too," said Kate, "but let's wait for Peppino, I hear his voice outside."

Peppino appeared in the doorway and nodded politely to the three of them. "There is a man here to see Mr. Farrell," he said.

"What man?" asked a startled Farrell.

Peppino stepped aside to allow passage, and Mr. Ambrose Vica entered the kitchen, blinking owlishly at the sudden brightness.

Farrell's mouth literally dropped open. "*You?*" he gasped. "But how—?"

Kate said sharply, "Peppi, how did this man get in? There was to be a guard at both the gates, you know that."

Peppino only smiled. "He is here, Caterina."

"Interesting," murmured Mrs. Pollifax, and was no longer at all sleepy.

Without preamble Ambrose Vica said, "Yes, I have come to see Mr. Farrell, who—ah, there you are, Farrell. Good evening—or should I say good morning?"

Farrell rose politely from his chair and then sank back. He said curtly, "One may ask how you learned where I am? I was going to phone you last evening but circumstances intervened. I have to ask—it's extremely important—*how did you learn that I'm here?*"

Vica said dryly, "The man who informed me of your whereabouts is outside in my car at this present moment, he declined to accompany me. Is there a Mrs. Pollifax here?"

Mrs. Pollifax raised her hand. "Here."

"You?" He frowned. "But I've seen you— ah yes, of course, you brought to me at breakfast a message about Farrell, a wild tale indeed. Is anyone going to invite me to sit down?"

"No," said Mrs. Pollifax. "Who is this man who told you where we are?"

He said testily, "No one is going to invite me to be seated?"

"Tit for tat," said Mrs. Pollifax pleasantly.

Vica's glance met hers and held it. He said sternly, "He tells me that you are the person, unbelievable as it may be, who rendered him unconscious on the grounds of my villa."

Kate laughed.

"*That* man?" asked Mrs. Pollifax in surprise. "But how would *he* know where I am?"

"He has given me his confidence," Vica said stiffly. "After all, he has been occupying a bed in my villa since the accident, and it became necessary for him to use my telephone to make a call to the United States. It seems that he has been following you, having been instructed in New York to keep you under constant surveillance."

"Impossible!" said Mrs. Pollifax indignantly.

"I believe him," said Vica. "His instructions, he tells me, came from a man named Bishop."

"Bishop?" faltered Mrs. Pollifax.

"The name is perhaps familiar to you?"

"But—but why on earth would I be placed under surveillance?" she stammered.

Farrell chuckled. "Carstairs' blood pressure? Certain past experiences recalled? His name is Henry, isn't it?"

"Henry Guise, yes. The poor man is afraid to leave my car outside until I have explained his presence, he's had a most difficult time of it. It seems that you incapacitated his car when he followed you out of Erice—"

"The gray one!" cried Kate.

"—and then, having lost you, he was instructed to watch for you at my villa, where of course you knocked him unconscious, and he now struggles to deliver a message to you from this—this Bishop. At the Villa Franca."

Farrell nodded. "So you asked directions from the post office, and—"

"On the contrary," Vica said, "I am quite familiar with the Villa Franca."

"And how is that?" said Farrell suspiciously.

"Never mind, what's the message?" asked Mrs. Pollifax.

Vica nodded. "Guise will be more precise when you meet him but the message was that a man by the name of Aristotle is no longer in prison and that you are to contact this Bishop at once."

"Oh, *that,*" said Mrs. Pollifax, disappointed.

"Yes, that." Turning to Farrell, Vica said, "But I have not yet learned what I particularly wish to know; I want to hear from you personally why—having engaged you to work for me—I have neither seen nor heard from you for— Ah, good evening, Franca."

Kate said in astonishment, "You *know* each other?"

Franca looked amused. "We've met, yes, but why have they kept you standing? Shame on you, Kate, offer Mr. Vica a chair and some coffee."

"But Franca, you don't understand the situation," protested Kate.

"Then let us learn what the situation is," she said firmly. "Over coffee. Unless the living room is preferred?"

"You have a very depressing living room," said Mr. Vica, and sat down in the chair that Mrs. Pollifax pulled out for him. "I am in the process, Franca, of extracting from this apparent guest of yours, Mr. Farrell, why he has not returned to my house for many days."

Farrell said indignantly, "I wanted to make a second try for the Caesar document you hired me to find and authenticate, and I did make a second try."

Vica said with sarcasm, "Very noble of you but it in no way answers the question.

Did you get *anything* from the safe in either attempt?"

Farrell nodded. "Yes, but nothing of consequence, you can see for yourself." He pushed back his chair and disappeared down the hall while Franca peered into the saucepan on the stove.

"Not coffee, this is cocoa."

"I will accept cocoa," said Mr. Vica with a faint smile.

He did not look a man who smiled often and Mrs. Pollifax, studying his sallow face, conceded that his smile made him look less thuglike.

Farrell returned and tossed on the table the contents of the safe that he'd been able to snatch on his first visit. Vica, leaning over them, suddenly smiled; it was his second smile. "Why didn't you tell me you'd secured these?"

"Because," said Farrell patiently, "it's the signature of Julius Caesar you hoped I'd find and sent me there to find." With a glance at Vica's changed face he said suspiciously, "Or was it?"

Vica picked up the small framed daguerreotype, turned it over and loosened the nails that held the photo in place. They watched in horror as he ripped out the photo. Holding up the sheet behind it he said, "Here is your signature of Julius Caesar. Authentic papyrus, Roman seal and signature."

Mrs. Pollifax gasped. "You mean—but how did you know it was behind the photo of that child?"

"Because I put it there."

"What the devil!" exploded Farrell.

"It's a forgery," Vica said. "Do you want to tell them, Franca, or shall I?"

"I think they already know," Franca said, looking amused.

"This is what I wanted," said Vica, picking out the sheet of names with its mysterious numbers. "Osepchuk, Champillion, Schweinfurth . . ." He nodded. "This is what I hoped you would find for me, Farrell. I trusted you to find it, I researched you thoroughly before hiring you: your years of experience with the Central Intelligence Agency, your capabilities, the fact that you're tough, resourceful, intelligent. But I still do not understand why you did not re-

turn to my house after opening Raphael's safe and finding these papers."

Farrell said in horror, "You *used* me like that? You didn't hire me for my art expertise? You took me on to rifle safes, get shot at and steal this page of names? *You're* the Second Thief," he said bitterly. "You sat back and let everyone else make damn fools of themselves when all the time—who the hell are you?"

"It scarcely matters," Vica said. "What matters is this list of names."

"And *not* the Caesar signature?" Kate said incredulously. "Why?"

Vica smiled. "Bait, my dear, bait. I had to protect myself, avoid the slightest suspicion. There had to be something to use as cover—Raphael is a dangerous man. He is also," he added, "an avid collector of ancient Greek and Roman artifacts."

"And are *you* a dangerous man?" asked Mrs. Pollifax with interest.

He said dryly, "Apparently—alas—I am only a 'Second Thief.' I see that you're looking at the document. It is a beautifully rendered forgery, masterfully done but with a deliberate and minute flaw that only X-rays could detect. Its existence was made known to Raphael through channels; he was quietly told of its discovery by a dealer in Rome with whom I placed it; he took the bait and bought it, whereupon rumors circulated that he had it, as they always do. It needed time, but I could wait, I knew that he would soon learn it was a forgery and would want to sell, and as a collector myself it was only natural that I approach him. He is not," he added pointedly, "an easy man to approach. When did you create this for me, Franca?"

"Eight or nine months ago."

He nodded. "Now I repeat: *why didn't you return to me, Farrell, after opening Raphael's safe?*"

Farrell said angrily, "Because two gunmen were waiting for me at Raphael's. Because I dared not trust you. Because of the man and woman I met at your house nine days ago, a man named Davidson—*especially* because of him."

"What, that boring chap?" said Vica in surprise. "They were luncheon guests, Raphael sent them."

"Why? What for?" demanded Farrell.

Vica's brows lifted. "My dear man, why such interest? I had intended to rent my villa for the summer months and go to Paris. They were prospective tenants. It was Raphael who told me that he knew of a couple—English I believe he said—who were looking for just such a place as mine for a few months. He offered to introduce them to me; I invited them and Raphael to lunch, Raphael was unable to come, so the Davidsons came alone. I showed them around, we had a most delicious lunch—my cook is superb—during which the Davidson's scarcely spoke a word. They had *no* conversation, which I found positively barbaric, I was forced to do all the talking. It turned out they—no, she—had a plane to catch later. When I learned of this—and the reason for it—I was able to extend my sympathies and the woman thawed somewhat, even weeping over this mother whom she'd not seen for years. It was all quite tedious, but of what possible interest can this drab couple be to you?"

Mrs. Pollifax said with feeling, "Because your drab Mr. Davidson happens to be a criminal of some note, lately released from prison in France, and since both Farrell and I were involved in *sending* him to that prison there have been a number of people chasing us, trying to shoot us, and in general being very tiresome.''

Startled, Vica said, "I see . . . I didn't realize.''

"And if I may interrupt this interrogation of Farrell,'' she went on, "I would very much like to know about this connection of yours with Franca and how you learned—''

"Of her paintings?'' he said smoothly, and gave Franca an amused glance. "It seems a fair question. It happened that we shared the same art dealer in Palermo. A bit of a rascal—it is wise to never *never* ask where or how he finds the very remarkable treasures that he presents. He announced one day—about ten years ago, wasn't it, Franca?—that he had discovered in someone's attic in Naples a portrait that he was sure was a Bellini.''

Farrell whistled through his teeth at this. "A Bellini!''

Vica nodded. "I bought it, had it examined and tested, and learned that it was a very clever forgery. Franca,'' he added parenthetically, "had not as yet fully developed her technique. When I decided to keep it anyway, I used considerable—shall we say pressure?—to persuade the dealer to tell me who had painted it, after which it amused me to pay a call on the Villa Franca." He sighed. "Since then I have purchased two of her—shall I say copies?—a Matisse and a Braque, to keep her out of trouble." Turning to her he said, "I don't like to ask how many you've completed that I don't know about. You refuse to consider the dangers, Franca."

"There was a Correggio," Farrell said musingly. "Absolutely gorgeous. It was in her office two days ago but has since disappeared."

Vica shook his head sadly. "Franca, you're *obsessed* with being independent and supporting the village. You can't do it from prison, you know, and it's only a matter of time before you're exposed. I beg of you again to consider retiring from all this, and marrying."

"*Marrying?*" said Kate. "Like who?"

Vica said with dignity, "I have proposed marriage to Franca at least three times a year for the past five years. She makes it very difficult even to see her, in fact I have once or twice had to bribe Peppino to get through the gates. She tells me that she esteems me, even though I am—as she says —an idle man of wealth, and a hedonist, she is grateful for my interest but values her independence. She continues to refuse me."

Three heads swiveled toward Franca, who said in an amused voice, "The alternative being prison?"

"God knows I am not an attractive man," Vica said, "but I have more money than I know what to do with and it is surprising how meaningless wealth can be with no one to share it with; I am frankly a lonely man. Peppino could take over from you here—he's an excellent man, Franca, you know that. You also know you need a rest from such responsibility. Fifteen years! Admit that you're bored, you're so bored you've begun changing the color of your hair every day!"

At this Franca gave him a sharp glance but said nothing.

"However," he said firmly, "this is neither

the time nor the place to propose marriage to a romantic woman—as you are, Franca, you are—so let us return to the business at hand. I would appreciate it if one of you would now be so kind as to conduct me to the cellar where I understand you have been hiding this Aristotle—who apparently I've already met as Davidson.''

He seemed surprised to find them all staring at him in horror. Kate stammered, ''But—Aristotle here? Wh-what can you mean?''

He said patiently, ''What I mean is that you have found the man—just in time—and we have found this list of names just in time.''

''In time for what—and who is 'we'?'' asked Farrell in a hard voice.

Vica's brows lifted. ''Interpol, of course.''

''*You're* Interpol?''

''You're *Interpol!*'' gasped Kate.

He shrugged. ''Let us say that I have a *connection* with them, that in my travels, and with my position, I have access to many people who are of great interest to Interpol, and learn many details that are of use. One likes to be useful," he said with a dry smile.

Franca looked at him accusingly. "I didn't know this."

He acknowledged this with an ironic bow. "One is not supposed to know, it pains me to mention it even now."

"Why didn't you tell us this immediately?" asked Mrs. Pollifax. "Of course it's been delicious, learning that Franca has a suitor, but I have to point out that you've been the villain of this piece at least until last night."

He raised his hand authoritatively. "Please—the suspicion has not been one-sided," he said, interrupting her. "It has been vital that I first learn Farrell's reasons for avoiding me. My dear Farrell, you have been under *considerable* suspicion for disappearing so abruptly as you did. Raphael has been known to corrupt some very respectable people, and for all I knew you had met Raphael when you went to—er—examine his safe, and he had bribed or persuaded you to work for him."

Kate said, "How *dare* you suspect Farrell!"

"Bless you, my dear," said Farrell, "I do appreciate your indignation." To Vica he said seriously, "I assume you can prove who you are?"

Vica looked amused. "Only by calling in the police, who wait patiently outside in four cars to remove Aristotle from your cellar . . . I am what you call the advance guard. There is another contingent in Palermo at the airport, prepared to transport him to France."

"He won't like there being so many," pointed out Mrs. Pollifax. "He doesn't like people."

"Sufficient punishment, then," said Vica.

"But he mustn't be found in the cellar," Kate said, quickly rising out of her chair. "Peppino, we must bring him upstairs— must—*at once!* You still have your gun with you?"

Vica, for the first time, looked puzzled. "Not found in the cellar?"

Apparently there was one secret about the Villa Franca that Ambrose Vica didn't know, and to distract him as Kate and Peppino left the room Mrs. Pollifax said, "I think we have a right to know what's behind this list of names that you've worked for so many months to find."

He said with distaste, "What lies behind these names is death. This Albert Raphael is a man who sells it, he deals in illegal arms transactions—riot guns, ammunition, Scuds, nuclear weapon materials, missiles of any type—whatever is forbidden export or import to whoever has money to buy: Africa, the Middle East, Balkans, Europe, terrorists anywhere." His lips tightened. "More dangerous even than this, however, was Interpol learning some eighteen months ago that Raphael had organized his various high-level contacts across the world into a tight group—a cartel of death, you might call it—and it is no less than that. The men in this select group of Raphael's have been unknown to us until now—at this moment—when I hold in my hand the list of their names and addresses. When I look at it—" He shook his head. "I scarcely need the addresses, these names—"

"You recognize them?" said Farrell quietly.

Vica nodded. "Sadly, yes. All but one or two of them are known and trusted men—I told you of Raphael's persuasive talents. It is a matter of deep disillusionment to see that such men in responsible positions have been so corrupted, involving themselves in providing the means to make wars, revolutions, coups."

"And Aristotle?" asked Mrs. Pollifax.

He shrugged. "Obviously they demanded the best, and were willing to go to any extreme to get it. Recently Interpol learned from an informant that the group had completed plans to murder—assassinate—a list of people who have gotten in their way, in particular those in government and investigative branches who have become outraged at corruption that can no longer be tolerated, people who have proven very inconvenient to such power-driven men as these . . . thus Aristotle."

"Whose reputation they knew, but not the man," said Mrs. Pollifax dryly.

They watched in silence as Vica scanned the list. He said, "I would suspect Champillion of being the most heavily involved in Aristotle's pardon from prison, he has that kind of influence in France. Osepchuk—a tricky politician in the Balkans who promotes nationalistic ambitions that lead, of course, to the arming of two sides at once and a doubling of profits."

Mrs. Pollifax shivered. "Certainly the world has never seemed more divided. Are you implying—"

"I am more than implying," said Vica. "To provide arms to just one fanatic, or to insinuate just one of these men or their hirelings into a position where advantage can be taken of an explosive situation is to apply a match to the proverbial tinderbox. Brother fights brother, tribe fights tribe and men grow rich from it." He said with contempt, "And Raphael doubtless buys a bigger yacht and a man like Osepchuk takes another mistress. But Champillion—" He shook his head. "It terrifies me to see his name linked with this cartel of death, he is known to be a member of numerous organizations for peace, a collector of fine art, and of rare books, a man of sensitivity and—you must forgive me but I have been personally involved in this search for the men Raphael had enlisted for his purposes and I can scarcely believe what I see on this list. We have indeed been in great danger in this world."

"You said Raphael was in oil?" Farrell reminded him.

The lamp over Vica flickered, shadowing his face for a moment. "Mere camouflage," he said. "It was the BCCI bank scandal that brought his name to the surface. His was one of many names, and seemingly of little importance until rumors and facts from various intelligence agencies around the world were pieced together and it was realized that Raphael is the shadow-figure behind arms smuggling that Interpol has known existed but couldn't trace."

"And now you've bagged him," said Farrell. "What will happen to Raphael and his merry group of murderers, if one may ask?"

Vica nodded. "Due process will begin, slowly but irrevocably," he said. "Indictments, arraignments, batteries of lawyers . . . Soon you will read a little of it in your newspapers and perhaps later, if it has some drama, you may hear of it on your television news. It will not interest many, I fear."

They were silent, hearing footsteps and

voices in the hallway: Peppino and Kate were returning from the cellar with Aristotle. As they entered the kitchen Vica rose from his chair. "So this is Aristotle," he said, "or should I say Mr. Davidson?"

Aristotle gave no evidence of recognizing him; his face remained expressionless, his eyes stony.

"Shall we go?" suggested Farrell, taking Peppino's place as guard.

Vica nodded and moved toward the door but Mrs. Pollifax had something to say. "Mr. Bimms—?"

He turned to look at her.

"For myself," she said, "I want to thank you for escaping Raphael and coming to us. If you hadn't—" She left the rest unsaid, and expecting no response she received none. He was a man who would have been happy to plan more killings if given a computer and a slide rule, he would have welcomed another opportunity to calculate trajectory, distance, the right weapon, the perfect disguise, the perfect shot and the getaway if Raphael had only understood his monomania. Ironically it was the sickest aspect of Aristotle's character that Mrs. Pollifax felt compelled to thank; it was this, after all, that had led to his rebellion.

Vica and Farrell escorted him out of the room and Kate followed, leaving Peppino, Franca and Mrs. Pollifax at a table strewn with empty cocoa cups.

"So," Peppino said with relief, "it is over?"

"Yes," said Mrs. Pollifax. "Exit Aristotle."

"So many men outside!" confided Peppino. "They didn't understand a word of Italian, those were not Palermo police. What is this Interpol?"

"The International Criminal Police Organization," explained Mrs. Pollifax.

Franca was smothering a yawn. "I'm suddenly rather tired," she said. "It's been a strenuous day. I've harbored a ruthless assassin in the cellar since morning, sliced two pounds of tomatoes, helped fight off a small army of hoodlums this evening, and received a proposal of marriage. Isn't anyone going to go to bed tonight?"

16

Overnight, calm appeared to have settled over the Villa Franca, and with it a slackening of its rituals: in the morning when Mrs. Pollifax arrived in the kitchen Igeia was nowhere to be seen, nor was the table set for breakfast. Someone had brewed coffee, however, and Mrs. Pollifax cut a slab of bread from the loaf on the counter, poured herself a cup of lukewarm coffee and retired to the garden to sort out the events of the past evening. There was much to think about: after all, her assignment to help Farrell had ended during the last night and this afternoon she would have to make arrangements to fly home.

Plucking a leaf of tarragon from the herb bed she found its summer fragrance as enchanting as always, and she thought that in her memory the Villa Franca was going to hold a fragrance very much like tarragon; she was going to miss it. Leaving, she would return again to a world of instant communication, to hot water that flowed at the twist of a faucet, to lights that sprang on at the touch of a switch, telephones that rang, and a society that moved too quickly to offer the sense of community that existed here. The contrast would be startling.

But she did hope that Franca would stop forging masterpieces before she was caught at it. Mr. Vica had been right about that. Mr. Vica, in fact, had been full of surprises.

She thought now of his description of Raphael's group as a cartel of death, and although the morning sun was dissipating the night's coolness she shivered. How impatient, she thought, how disgusted with the greatest protection civilization possessed—the law—and how arrogant their determination to have their own way and kill to achieve it.

Have their own way . . .

She remembered an incident with her son Roger—had he been four years old or five? —when he had stood rooted and furious in the backyard after breaking the toy of a playmate. He'd shouted to her, "He got in my way—I could kill him!" If Roger had been too young to understand the words he'd shouted, his primitive fury at that moment had been real. He had wanted his own way.

As these men did now.

Except they were not five years old.

And again she shivered, hoping the law would not move *too* slowly.

Behind her in the kitchen she heard voices raised in argument and she smiled ruefully: Kate and Farrell, of course, and she frankly eavesdropped.

"Of course I want my coffee black," snapped Kate. "Surely you've noticed that by now?"

"Why so cross, for pete's sake?" asked Farrell. "All's well that ends well, Aristotle's on his way back to the prison cell he never wanted to leave, Ambrose Vica has his list—"

"Yes, and Mr. Vica will stop in this afternoon to give you a fat check and talk to Franca, and then you'll fly off tomorrow and forget about you and me?"

There was a silence, a very long silence, and Mrs. Pollifax thought, *Oh dear, Farrell's panicked?*

When Farrell spoke again his voice was sober. "It won't work, you know, Kate."

"Won't work! Do you mind telling me why?" demanded Kate.

"Because I can't ask you to give up your work with the Department, and because I think you'd find life in an art gallery damnably dull, and because if you stayed with the Department I'd worry about you constantly. I've been there, you know, I've experienced it, I know the hazards. It can be *dangerous.*"

"Sarajevo was an exception," she told him. "I didn't expect it to turn into a killing ground."

"One never does. Or someone to poke a gun in your ribs and say, I know who you are."

She said accusingly, "Is that why *you* retired?"

"There was an element of burnout, yes," he said, "but I'd also grown tired of concealing who I was after twenty years. You haven't reached that stage yet. Mostly, though, I wanted to find out what the real world was like, learn what else was possible, and live normally."

"Normally!" she flung at him. "So you ended up in Zambia working with the freedom fighters! Come off it, Farrell."

"You know that's not the way it was, I simply chose Zambia to raise cattle and to farm, and it just so happened—"

"Yes, just happened, and you were called Mulika, shedder of light, and risked your neck every *day*."

"And Sarajevo found you living in a cellar with bombs exploding all around you, and—"

"I think," interrupted Kate, "that we're getting off the subject, aren't we? It would be rather nice to give *me* some choice in this matter, I don't appreciate being told how I'll feel or react. It's incredible—you actually plan to just fly off to Mexico City tomorrow, leaving me here to finish my rest-leave and go on to my next assignment, and we simply exchange Christmas cards every year?"

"Kate," he said, "listen to me. I'm fifteen years older than you, I'm forty-one, I've lived a rather rum life and done a lot of rum things and you deserve better."

"Really? Then can you tell me where on earth I'll find someone exactly like you but fifteen years younger? Of course you're being gallant, I see that now," she added deliberately. "I have an aunt who may be arrested tomorrow—any day or year—and could be visited only in a prison, which would be enormously embarrassing for you."

Farrell laughed. "Deliver me from a clever woman! You know very well—"

"What I know very well is that what is between us is *good.* I love you, damn it, and you said you loved me, too, and I'd appreciate being *asked* my thoughts on the matter, not told it wouldn't work. You're scared, Farrell, admit it. Scared of commitment."

"I'm only thinking of you," protested Farrell.

"You're not thinking of me at all," she told him indignantly.

"Kate—stay away from me," Farrell said warningly. "You're not thinking of this sensibly and rationally, and—"

Another silence followed. Obviously Kate had moved into his arms, thought Mrs. Pollifax contentedly, and she left her chair to stroll over and examine the purple buds on the comfrey. A few minutes later, hearing Igeia's voice in the kitchen, she walked back into the house, hoping not only to learn the outcome of this rocky romance but also hoping for some breakfast.

She found Kate radiant; seeing her she said, "Mrs. Pollifax, I've another two weeks of leave and I'm going back with Farrell to Mexico City! To see his art gallery, and—"

"—and sort out possibilities," Farrell added, and with an impish grin he said, "Well, Duchess? She refuses to listen to reason, you know."

"I'm surprised you thought she would," said Mrs. Pollifax. "I'm delighted."

"Of course," added Farrell, "you realize that she *really* wants to research my gallery as an outlet for her aunt's forgeries."

"Presumptious man," said Kate. "Let's go and tell Franca, *she'll* be surprised."

Mrs. Pollifax doubted this very much.

*   *   *

Half an hour later, standing on the hill overlooking the village, Mrs. Pollifax saw Franca approaching and greeted her. "I've been enjoying the silence after last night's noisy interlude. Kate and Farrell have told you their news?"

Franca smiled. "Yes, and I fervently hope she'll find the art gallery stimulating and fun. I love her dearly and I've worried about her doing the work she's chosen. I think Farrell's very right for her, too."

"You weren't surprised, then."

Franca laughed. "He was so *very* cross when he arrived here, and Kate so *very* angry at him—quite unlike her!—that it made me suspicious at once."

"How perceptive! But Franca," she said, examining her with some surprise, "you're wearing your own hair today. No wig?"

She said vaguely, "Oh, that . . . no . . . so much has been happening . . . ."

"So Mr. Vica was right, then, about the

boredom? I hear he's coming back this afternoon."

Franca did not answer, she was staring down at the houses and the fields below, and from the expression on her face Mrs. Pollifax guessed that she was thinking of something very different. "There's so much of my history here," she said with a sigh. "So many years!"

At once Mrs. Pollifax understood what lay behind this retreat into the past. She said gently, "Tell me."

Franca hesitated and when she spoke again her voice held a somber, dreamy quality. "It's just that I've been remembering so much . . . how it all began—each family drawing lots for their four-acre parcels—and how that didn't work because, as you can imagine, the distance to some of the gardens was too far from the gates and the village, and the gardens farthest from the wells didn't prosper, which led to bad feeling . . ."

"How was *that* solved?" asked Mrs. Pollifax, curious.

"By blackmail, really," Franca said ruefully. "The greatest draw was promising a tractor—and the hope of a reservoir for water—and so the vote was finally to share all of the land. Food on the table is a great persuader," she added with a smile. "Also the fact that if the cooperative should ever fail they would still own their original four acres since the deeds are properly registered."

"I don't know how you found time to paint your canvasses!"

"Well," admitted Franca with a smile, "that is exactly why each canvas I painted had to eventually be so *extremely* remunerative . . . There was Nito, for instance, so bright a boy I feared we might lose him to the—the people one would not wish to lose him to in Sicily . . . With my second painting he was sent off to college. With the next one—nameless," she said quickly, "we bought the larger generator, and the tractor, and when Nito came home married to a schoolteacher we began the school . . . and by then the crops were doing so well, the earth rich at last, the men had time to dig at night under the house, and from selling a few of the artifacts that we excavated —stealthily, of course—we installed cisterns and the water systems." She sighed. "But it is no longer quite so exciting now, I admit."

"You mean you've been working yourself out of a job," Mrs. Pollifax told her sympathetically.

Franca's smile was rueful. "I have been a parent to the village, you understand? And there comes a time when a good parent lets go—yet it's been such a wonderful fifteen years for me." She turned to look at Mrs. Pollifax searchingly. "Do you think I can change at my age? Live a different life?"

And now we arrive at the nub of the matter, thought Mrs. Pollifax, and aloud she said, "We are speaking here of Ambrose Vica, I think. Who returns this afternoon, I hear?"

Franca nodded. "So he told Farrell last night when he left with your assassin." She said carefully, "It is true that he startled me —was it only last night? I had thought him only an idle man of no purpose. Always I have found him kind—but until last night I didn't realize *how* kind, I didn't know that it was he who bought the Matisse and the Braque to—to protect me. I have liked him, he has been honest and frank with me in his dealings, and I have seen his loneliness. But to be so rich—"

"You're afraid of ease?" asked Mrs. Pollifax.

"I admit this, yes," Franca said, nodding.

"But haven't you earned it?"

Franca shrugged. "One acquires habits," she said wryly. "The habit of being useful."

"That I can understand," Mrs. Pollifax told her, and added mischievously, "But think of how creatively you could encourage him to use his great fortune!"

Franca looked amused. "I'd not thought of that. He has power, that man! It would be —interesting, yes. But why do you think he wants to marry me?"

Mrs. Pollifax laughed. "Because you're both—well, I would say that both of you are outlaws in your different and unusual ways. You're his *equal,* Franca."

"Not in fortune."

"True," said Mrs. Pollifax, "but I can tell you that for myself, Franca, I also esteem and admire you. I can't judge you. I'm married to a man I love very much who upholds the law—he's a retired judge—and I've come to realize today that I dare not tell him about your Correggio and your other forgeries, and this will be the first secret that I've ever kept from him."

Franca said with interest, "He would arrest me, do you think?"

Mrs. Pollifax shook her head. "Oh no, but it would make him terribly uncomfortable, it would be a confidence that would *burden* him. It will have to remain *my* knowledge, *my* secret. It must."

"If that is true," Franca said gravely, "it is a great gift that you're giving me. Your silence."

"Possibly as a wedding gift?" said Mrs. Pollifax with a twinkle.

Franca laughed. "About that we will see. You give me good reasons to say yes to Ambrose, I think he comes to speak of this again today so I will think hard of what you said."

Mrs. Pollifax smiled. "Then I'll leave you to your thoughts and wish you good ones."

"Thank you, Mrs. Pollifax, or—Emily?"

"Emily's much better, yes," she told her, and left her to her reflections.

*   *   *

When they returned after lunch from the airport, with reservations for the morning flight to New York, there was a brown Fiat parked by the house. "That looks familiar," said Farrell. "It's Vica's car, the one I had to abandon in Erice."

As Kate drew up next to it, Mr. Vica walked out of the house looking dazed; glimpsing them he only nodded, climbed into his car and headed for the gates.

She's refused him, thought Mrs. Pollifax, and hurried ahead into the kitchen, wondering if she would find Franca melancholy or relieved. Instead Franca was seated at the table staring into space, and she looked as dazed as Mr. Vica had looked.

"Franca, we're back," she told her. "Ambrose Vica was here?"

Franca emerged from her trance with a curious smile tugging at her lips. "I said yes to him, Emily . . . We're going to be married in Paris. Next week—before I change my mind, he says."

Mrs. Pollifax chuckled; it was no wonder that Mr. Vica had looked dazed. "And you —are you happy about it?"

Franca regarded her thoughtfully. "It surprises me, but yes, I think I feel *very* happy about it. I will of course have to wear shoes," she said gravely, "but otherwise Ambrose says he does not wish me to change in the slightest way." She suddenly laughed. "He says I must even bring my wigs, that in Paris—if I wish—I may set a new style. I, set a new style!"

"I think I like this Ambrose Vica very much," said Mrs. Pollifax warmly, and mentally apologized to him for thinking he looked like a thug. Already in her mind a picture was forming of Franca in Paris, in New York, Rome, the Riviera, of people murmuring, "Look, there's that wonderfully eccentric Mrs. Vica—*not* a beauty for a change—but such an *original.*"

She liked that picture.

She liked equally well the thought that in forty-eight hours she would see Cyrus again. There would be so very much to tell him—but not everything, she remembered —at least not *quite* everything.

17

Two weeks later, back from Chicago for her birthday, Mrs. Pollifax received two interesting and unexpected messages. A cable from Mexico City was delivered while she and Cyrus were lingering over morning coffee. The cable read: SORRY TO REPORT MY CHARM FAILED ME. DUCHESS STOP KATE RETURNED TO WORK YESTERDAY BUT LEFT A SUITCASE FULL OF CLOTHES STOP QUERY IS THIS HOPEFUL STOP COME VISIT SOON AND CONSOLE ME YOU TWO STOP LOVE AND KISSES FARRELL.

"Doesn't sound *too* wounded," said Cyrus when she read it to him. "May even be relieved."

"One can never really tell," she said

thoughtfully, reading over the words again. "Neither of them were ready for this, I think, which is why they were both so angered— even hostile—about the attraction."

"Timing bad?" suggested Cyrus. .

She nodded. "It probably couldn't be worse. You have Kate, very ambitious, younger, and finally doing the work she's always wanted, and then you have Farrell, who has tired of that same work and has left it to settle down and enjoy his gallery." She smiled. "But the suitcase left behind is intriguing."

"Agreed," said Cyrus. "I *like* Farrell . . . A return cable with our sympathy, perhaps?"

"Definitely," she said, and had just completed sending it when the morning mail arrived, bearing a postcard with a picture of the Eiffel Tower.

"It's from Franca!" she exclaimed, and Cyrus put down his cup of coffee and waited.

Dear Emily, wrote Franca, *Paris has been wonderful. Not only are we buying works of promising (and starving!) artists but Ambrose is in touch with the United Nations about building and supporting a center for Balkan orphans and refugees. You are an even better witch than Norina, dear Mrs. P. . . . love, Franca.*

"A cup-runneth-over moment," she told Cyrus, handing the Paris card to him across the breakfast table.

Cyrus read it and said, "You were in Sicily less than a week—and this happened, too?"

Mrs. Pollifax said modestly, "It was a very *accelerated* week."

"And next," he said dryly, "we can expect a card from Aristotle telling us what a wonderful time *he's* having and wishing we were with him?"

Mrs. Pollifax laughed, and Cyrus returned to his newspaper but as he turned a page he added, "Only wish I could have seen some of Franca's work—rather odd nobody seems to have heard of her. Must have been outstanding to have supported an entire village as it did."

"It was outstanding, yes, but I'm not sure that it would have been quite to your taste," she told him truthfully, and felt that she had navigated her last shoal.

Until her birthday, that is, when Cyrus carried her off to New York City to celebrate it with a long weekend of theater, art exhibits, moviegoing and the luxury of not cooking a single meal. She found it extremely restful, except for one moment during the weekend when they visited the Metropolitan Museum, and the guide, sharing information with them, pointed to an alcove in which a single painting was displayed.

"That's the Frans Hals in there," he said. "Hung it just last week. Spent four years arguing whether it's authentic or fake but they settled it at last. You might want to take a look, it's quite a find."

"Frans Hals," she repeated, and suddenly she was remembering Farrell saying, *That Dutch painting four years ago, Franca —a Frans Hals, wasn't it? The experts are still arguing over it, some calling it genuine, others a forgery. Dare I ask—?*

And Franca confiding, *I always place a very tiny dot in one corner of each painting so that I'll recognize it in a museum.*

I don't want to look, thought Mrs. Pollifax, *I don't want to know.* "If you don't mind, Cyrus, I'd rather not," she said. "We've

seen so much that I'm experiencing over-
load, and isn't it nearly time for lunch? I'm
famished."

Cyrus gave her an amused glance.
"Amazing how many paintings are being
forged these days, isn't it?" With a faint
smile—as if he knew exactly why she preferred not to see the painting—he said,
"Then of course we'll forego the Frans Hals
and have lunch, my dear."

*   *   *